IT ALL STARTED
WITH A NEW JOB

IT ALL STARTED WITH A NEW JOB

D. MORGAN

authorHOUSE®

AuthorHouse™ UK Ltd.
1663 Liberty Drive
Bloomington, IN 47403 USA
www.authorhouse.co.uk
Phone: 0800.197.4150

Published by AuthorHouse   07/10/2013

ISBN: 978-1-4817-7538-0 (sc)
ISBN: 978-1-4817-7539-7 (e)

Dedication

I was lucky that my twin brother and I were brought
into this world by two very special people who asked
for nothing, but yet gave everything that mattered
unconditionally.
No matter how bad things seemed at times, they were
always there for all of us.
I feel so sad that I don't have my solid brick walls as a
cushion anymore, but I am so lucky and honoured to
have shared a big part of they're lives and hold the special
memories of these two unbelievable people that I will
always cherish.
If you knew them you loved them.
I miss you both so much and want to thank you for
everything.

David

I dedicate this book to Glyn and Grace Morgan
(My Mam & Dad)

We all have experienced in life a nagging sense that we should have turned right instead of left.

Fate is sometimes your worst nightmare and regularly makes decisions for you. It's not your fault, sometimes that's just the way it is.

Christopher Evans was just a normal average everyday guy, making his way through life the best way he could and was doing fine.

By accident he is witness to two innocent people murdered by the leader of a smuggling ring.

This was done in cold blood and in front of him.

His past comes back to haunt him. Was it by chance?

The feeling of hatred, plus the need for revenge is taking him over.

He gets his chance. But everything comes with a price.

His journey takes him from the U.K. to Malaysia and Singapore.

He has no choice but to put his trust in people that want this man as bad as he does.

CHAPTER 1

As I ran into my office I did not know what hit me. There was a flash and a force that threw me back against the wall like a rag doll. It was followed by a loud explosion that felt so violent and terrifying. I remember being hit by flying shrapnel and the feeling as it embedded itself into my ribs and cheek. The pain was intense and I passed out. I can feel myself coming around.

I don't know how long I had been out of it. I am lying on my side, my right arm is behind me twitching spasmodically, my right cheek is on the floor and I can feel warm blood trickling down my face and pooling around my mouth. My mouth is open bubbling the blood as I breathe out. My eyes are closed and there's a very sharp pain in my ribs. I can't speak. I am trying to call out 'help me' but nothing is happening. I'm very frightened, I can't move, somebody please help me.

Through the ringing in my ears I can hear a fire alarm, or an ambulance, or . . . something. Yes, it's a siren! It's help! Please, for God's sake somebody help me. I am trying to open my eyes. Yes! I can move them! I am slowly focusing.

I can see the shape of the office door. I can make out the figure of a man standing there. He is walking towards me . . . Oh no! He has a gun in his hand! He is pointing it at me. He's going to shoot me. I can see that the gun is a browning. All I can do is focus on that gun. I can see every contour of it. He's wearing ring on his index finger. It's a gold ring with an insignia forged into it; a shape (刃). I recognize it . . . the bastards have found me!

"Somebody, please!" nothing is coming out, what can I do?

'There is somebody in here get a medic quickly.' The call by a security guard saved my life. The gun was withdrawn as the man shouted,

'He's hurt, help him.'

I noticed that he had an oriental sound to his voice. I am trying hard to focus on his face but my vision is still a bit blurry. I can make out dark skin, and Asian-looking eyes. Suddenly, he retreated through the door and disappeared. I can't believe what has happened to me in the past year. It all started with a new job.

(Previously)

The alarm went off with a buzz that seemed to get louder every morning. I did my usual routine of throwing my shoe at it and swearing.

'You bad tempered old fart!' came a voice from beside me, 'you really are a grouch in the mornings Chris, it must be your age!'

Samantha (or Sam as she prefers to be known) is younger than me. She's in her early twenties in fact. I'm thirty two (which I consider to be an acceptable age gap although my mates still insist that I'm a dirty old man! I know that they are just jealous!) Sam has been a godsend to me. I have encountered a few problems in my life but she really has helped me to sort myself out. She's a gorgeous looking girl; soft brown skin, big almond-shaped eyes and a big heart. She comes from an English born white mother, and an Indian born dad, hence her beautiful skin tone. She wears my old T-shirts to bed yet still manages to make them look like something that Armani would be proud of.

She got out of bed and walked across the room to turn the alarm clock off,

'I thought you put the clock over there so you would have to get out you lazy bastard! And you had better get a wriggle on, you can't be late on your first day. Your boss won't like that.'

She gave me a peck on the cheek and went to her room (or where she should stay) in the flat across the hall. She shared the flat with two other students, all of them studying in Cardiff University.

They had lived there for nearly a year. Sam and I seemed to hit it off from the start. She would come around to use my computer, then stay longer than she ought to. I think that she's glad to have a break from the other girls, especially when they have their wild parties. Her father seems to be strict. He would probably have my balls for breakfast if he knew what was going on between us, but *what daddy doesn't know, won't hurt him and I am not going to tell him am I!*

I got out of my nice, comfortable, cozy bed and walked towards the bathroom. I passed the picture of my son Andrew (he's six next month.) I really miss him. I miss simple things; like putting him to bed every night, wiping his runny nose and playing on the Game boy together. I should be looking forward to today. It's Monday. A new job and a fresh start, but Mondays hold bad memories. Well, one does in particular . . .

Two years ago I drove to work, walked up to my office door, and realized that I had forgotten the drawings for a new shopping precinct being built in Cardiff. The meeting for the job was at ten, though I didn't consider that to be a problem as there was a spare set printed out in Mark's office . . . but Mark wasn't in. His office was locked and there were no spare keys. My only option was to go back home and pick up my copies. When I got there I found Mark's car on my drive, Mark's shoes and keys at the bottom of my stairs and Mark in bed with Jayne my wife. I lost it completely. I regret how badly I hurt him. I just freaked out. I threw him out without anything on, and the only thing that he had to cover himself was his car keys and shoes that I tossed at him. The neighbors found it quite amusing!

I collected some of Andrews's clothes and took him to a friend's house to stay. It was fine for a while but Andrew was really missing his mother. I just couldn't do that to him no matter what I thought of her, so we came to an amicable arrangement. The only problem being that Mark (or dickhead as I affectionately call him) had moved in. He's good to Andrew but he is never going to call him Dad, I will make sure of that.

Anyway, go forwards not backwards as Sam keeps telling me. The world's your lobster as she said once when I was a bit low! With her behind me I feel a lot more confident. A last look in the mirror, straighten my tie and let's go for it big time! Sam heard me closing my door and came out of her flat.

'Have a nice day at the office darling!' she said, taking the piss as usual. She gave me an over-exuberant peck on the cheek. I picked up my letters; more bills, then I climbed into my old faithful black Golf Gti. I drove to work, mentally running through everything that had happened to me in the past, and then consoled myself with thoughts of my new future.

CHAPTER 2

I left school before completing my A levels. My parents had high hopes for me but I failed to get onto my chosen course at university. I had so many arguments with them: it was *my* life and *I* will choose what I want to do with it! It ended with my father (who was a very strict, and sometimes a very violent man) throwing me out. I was just eighteen. I could fight the world on my own! I decided to join the Army. They accepted me and I joined the Royal Engineers. Everything was going well and I even signed up for a longer stint. It wasn't until I got stationed at RAF Bruggen in Germany that problems started to arise.

My mate Jimmy accidentally witnessed a scam that had been going on for a while. It seems that a few of the guys were involved in a very well organized drug smuggling racket. Jimmy came across them one night by accident. He had found a way of sneaking in and out of the airbase without being spotted. He would go and see his girlfriend Heike in the near-by village for a quick one, and then return before anybody had even noticed he was gone.

One night he came back past one of the Hercules aircraft just in from Afghanistan and found that the tailgate was down. Two guys were inside, pulling bags of white powder out of a Land Rover's spare wheel. He tip-toed away without anybody noticing (or so he thought) and told me. Early the next morning, Jimmy said that he had received orders to leave and join another regiment in Cyprus. He left. My curiosity got the better of me that night. Another Hercules was flying in from Afghanistan so I thought that I would have a look for myself. Jimmy had told me of his hiding place (just off the runway where there was a good view of everything). Even the SAS would have been proud of him! Sure enough, I could see right into the tail of the plane. Two M.P. sergeants were unloading a spare tyre from one of the 4x4 armored vehicles. They started pulling out bags of white powder from it. My god, he was right!

I had a good check around. I couldn't see anybody about so I headed back to the barracks with the intention of telling my C.O.

Just as I reached the door, two heavy's wearing M.P. uniforms confronted me. As I turned to go the other way, two more came from behind.

'Oh look what we've found!' gloated the big black guy with no neck,

'You shouldn't be out at this time of night, I think we'll have to do something about this'

He was enormous. He made Tyson look like a ballet dancer! As one thug cable tied my hands the other hit me in the ribs so hard that I thought I would die right there and then. They threw me in the back of their Land Rover, blindfolded me and drove off out of the camp to somewhere about ten minutes away (at least it seemed like ten minutes anyway.) Once there, they took great delight in throwing me out onto the hard gravel surface face first. As my head scraped along the floor the blindfold moved slightly. I remember it stung like hell. They dragged me into somewhere cold and threw me down again. I could see a whitewashed room with a single bulb hanging from the ceiling. I lay on a plain concrete floor that smelt of piss. They kicked the shit out of me until I passed out.

I came around as icy-cold water was thrown over me. I didn't know how long I had been unconscious. I had a thumping headache. I hurt all over and I was shaking with the cold. Two men picked me up, dragged me to another room and sat me in a chair.

'Where am I and what's happening'?

Somebody punched me in the face.

'Shut up and don't speak unless you are spoken to you prick!'

They walked out of the room and left me there alone, cuffed and blindfolded. I was too afraid to move just in case I would get another beating. I guess ten minutes must have passed when the door opened. I sensed that they were dragging in two people. Once they had sat them down they took my blindfold off. The bright light and white washed walls felt as if they were burning holes in my eyes.

As my vision focused I realized that I was in another plain white room. It was about six meters by twelve meters with Halogen lights on all the walls and some storage racks. It must have been some kind of old store room. Next to me was a very swollen-faced Jimmy and Heike (his girlfriend) sat next to him. She looked scared to death and sobbed uncontrollably. All of the men in the room wore M.P. uniforms. The lump of a bloke that cuffed me started shouting,

'We want to know who have you been talking to and what you know!'

I could not believe something like this could happen in the British forces and at an airbase. He kicked off,

'Who the Fuck have you been talking to!'

He hit Jimmy off his seat, driving the full force of his fist to the side of his head. Some blood (along with one of his teeth) flew out of his mouth as if in slow motion. Two other guards helped him back in the chair.

'You will tell us you piece of shit!'

I raised my head slightly as somebody walked in the room. He was a Chinese guy, stocky with a well-tanned face. He had very menacing looking eyes. He wore a long raincoat buttoned up fully; it seemed to be concealing something. He had one hell of a shiny ring on his right index finger. It was bright gold and it had a (刃) emblem on it. I overheard one of the guards,

'Why don't we just fucking waste them and get it over with.'

All I thought was that we had seen their faces, so we are going to die. Another guy came in to the room. He was wearing an R.A.F. flight lieutenant uniform; a very clean-shaven slim man, well in his fifties. He wore the same ring. I heard them just call the Chinese guy boss. He walked up to Jimmy, then without hesitation opened up his raincoat revealing a gun. He put the gun to Jimmy's head,

'You had better start talking very quickly. Who do you work for?'

Jimmy replied, crying as he spoke,

'I don't know what the Fuck you are on about! Please just let us go, we won't say anything'

The Chinese guy had a 9mm Glock pointed point blank at him. He moved the gun to Heiker's head. There was a loud bang. Both Jimmy and I were splattered with bits of Heiker's brains. He turned to Jimmy,

'Do not waste your time boys. We have more important things to do.'

He shot Jimmy in the head without any sign of remorse or hesitation. I didn't even hear the gun go off I was still deaf from the last shot. I was in shock, all I could think was *I am next*. I felt warm piss running down my leg. I think I cried out something while physically shaking with fear, waiting for my turn.

They pulled my sleeve up and stabbed a needle into my arm, Sodium Pentothal type stuff I thought. I prayed that I would be released if they believed my story. It didn't take long for me to start feeling like I was in a tunnel. Every sound was becoming an echo. I pretended that I was passing out. My sight became a bit blurred but I could still make out the voice shouting at me,

'Who are you working for?'

Another voice in the background said,

'You stupid bastard, you have given him too much, look at him he's fucked up!'

'Shoot him and let's go'

I kept exaggerating my condition, trying to get a few more seconds of life. I didn't want to die. The whole room lit up as a flash grenade went off. There was a bright flash, followed by a loud bang, then the phut-phut sound of guns double tapping as they hit their targets. Some of the bullets seemed to be flying all over the place, pinging of the walls chaotically. Then there was a perfect silence. It seemed to last for ages but in reality was only seconds. My ears were ringing and I was temporarily blinded from the grenade. I was also cold and stunk of piss but at least I was alive.

As my sight returned I could see that some men had entered. They were dressed in black and wearing gas masks. They had shot and killed almost everybody in the room with pin-point accuracy, except me, the Pilot and the Chinese guy; they shot him in the arm.

They cut off the cable tie on my wrist and I got up, but I was still wobbly. I put all my weight on the guys holding me up. While two other SAS guys restrained the Chinese man. I gave him a good, hard kick in the balls! That alone was a feat with all that shit they had pumped into me. In reality I may not have hit him that hard but I did it. They were quick to take us away from the place. I screamed at the Asian; I was full of adrenalin and whatever shit that was they had pumped into me,

'I'm going to kill you! You bastard! I'll Fucking kill you!'

I don't know where they took him. I passed out. I awoke to find myself in a hospital bed with my wounds dressed. I didn't know what I had involved myself in but an armed guard had been stationed outside my room.

CHAPTER 3

The next morning I awoke feeling like shit. My ribs were killing me and my head felt like the Paddington train from Cardiff was in it. A nurse came in and took my temperature and blood pressure.

'Somebody's here to see you, are you feeling well enough for a visitor?'

Before I could say no, a man dressed in a grey suit walked in. He was about six three and slim with graying hair. He had sharp, chiseled features. It was hard to put an age on him but he looked in his fifties. He seemed very confident and carried himself well; obviously military. He sat down next to me. As the nurse left he shook my hand and introduced himself.

'My name is David Denton. I am here to help you. I am going to be your guardian angel for a while. I first need to tell you a few things about me and what has been going on, this is all classified you understand.'

I stared at him in disbelief, struggling to take in the recent events. He continued his speech regardless,

'I know that you still must be suffering from shock but it is a matter of urgency that you are flown back to Britain, a.s.a.p. I work for a government department within the MI6 bubble. We are very active in worldwide drug and smuggling operations. We work alongside other countries and their operations, to get rid of the bad boys so to speak. Luckily for you we have been watching this smuggling operation for a while.'

He walked around the bed, holding his lapels as he strode,

'They caught your friend watching them. Unfortunately, they are aware that were onto them. They must have assumed that he was an informant. You see, in Afghanistan it's funny how things have turned out. It was only a few years back the American's were helping a lot of the people that we are now fighting against. Some of our contacts from those days are still active and in touch. Never mind Alkaida and the fight against the West, greed and power still drive all organizations. Terrorist groups, the same as any other company, need funding. It's a priority. These people will use whatever means necessary in order to get what they want. I promise you, as soon we were aware that you and your friends had been captured the order was issued for a strike team to go in. We were getting ready to enter when the shooting started. I am so very sorry about your friends'

I looked at the floor through tear-filled eyes as a vivid flashback of their executions came over me. He continued,

'I have been setting this up for a long time. We have apprehended the ringleaders in Afghanistan. There is enough evidence to put them away for good. With your account of tonight's events we should be close to shutting down the whole operation. The Chinese man is known as Yip. He is a ringleader of the Asian wing of the organization. With this evidence we should be able to pin him with murder and drug smuggling.

He glanced at his wristwatch,

'We really do need to move you as soon as possible. I have an ambulance down stairs to take you to the airport. You will be taken to a safe house in the U.K.'

'What are you going to do with that Yip guy? And why is he here?'

'He is a link in the chain of this well organized drug smuggling operation. We have been watching him for two years. He owns an exporting company in the Far East and has been using it as a front to smuggle and recruited some of forces personnel. Hopefully, now we can put him and his partners out of business for good.'

With that I was taken away. After they had moved me back to the UK it took quite a while for them to get things sorted for the trial. I was moved from safe house to safe house as I was told that some of the key players in the whole thing were high-ranking officials. I had a price on my head. All I wanted was revenge for my mate and his girlfriend. I swear they won't get away with it.

The court case came and went. The accused were all found guilty and put away in some high security Military Prison. I heard that they had been sent to America but nobody seemed to know for sure, either that or they deliberately weren't telling me. As soon as the trial was over David came to see me and clarified a few things,

"We have to give you a new identity. The people who you have helped to lock up are well connected. Even though they are imprisoned they can still take their revenge. They are set to lose millions due to us destroying their business venture over here and abroad.'

I didn't care about that, I was still thinking about Jimmy and Heike. They gave me a new identity. I kept my first name. They said it was easier and normal when relocating people. Gone was Christopher Evans and hello Christopher Thomas. These guys really knew what they were doing. They gave me a birth certificate and passport. They also helped me to relocate to Caerphilly. My appearance was changed with a new haircut, glasses, and I lost a little weight. It was quite spooky seeing the new me in the mirror. Dave (as he preferred to be called) even set me up with a few thousand in the bank, a mortgage on a two-bedroom house and Engineering qualifications with my new name on them. They found me a new job with a local company where I met Jayne. We got married and had our son Andrew in a short space of time. Everything was going well for a while then things fell apart again.

I left the job after catching dickhead and Jayne together. He had a lot more friends at work than I did and they all seemed to side with him for some strange reason, even though I felt I was the one being hard done by. I chose to leave. I spent a while fucking up the drawings and quotes on his office computer first, of course, trying to drop him in the shit! I regretted that later.

Dave (my guardian angel) would show his face now and then to see how I was doing. When I thought everything was going to pieces again he was there to help. I had a lot to thank him for.

CHAPTER 4

I drove through Cardiff city center and towards the docks, wondering what my first day at work would bring. As I approached, I noticed that the dockland (which was once a run-down area) had been turned into either flats or offices. The whole area was a mixture of steel, glass, old brickwork and stone textured buildings that were once busy warehouses.

I drove towards the old dry dock and turned towards my new place of work then down a concrete ramp that led to a security gate. A man came out of a small security block with tinted windows, dressed in what could have passed for an American police uniform (except for the E.T. company logo on the lapel and hat badges.)

'Good morning sir we have been expecting you, could you drive straight through to the underground car park and park your car near to the lift. Exit the lift on the first floor and reception will sort you out.'

I noticed he was holding an A4 sheet of paper with a photograph of me and my details. I did as I was instructed. I couldn't help but notice the amount of security cameras everywhere; in the car park, the lift and at in the reception. I walked towards the reception desk where Nicky (the girl who was on my interview panel) greeted me with a smile. She seemed to know everything about the company. I have always thought that most secretaries know more about a business than their bosses!

I followed her into the lift and we exited on the second floor. We passed a security door (which led to an empty corridor) and entered an office. Jayne got up from behind her large mahogany desk and shook my hand. She was a very smart lady, a bit older than me, in her mid to late thirties and dressed very businesslike. She was blonde with a rounded face and very wide blue eyes. When she smiled cute dimples appeared on her cheeks. She was tall and slim, and as a red blooded male couldn't help noticing what a nice set of jugs she had!

The suit did nothing for her, and the buttons on her blouse pulled apart slightly when she stretched. I noticed (through the gap) that her bra was doing overtime to keep those beauties pointing in the right direction! I tried hard not to let her catch me looking. It reminded me of being back at school in a history lesson, hoping that Miss Jones would undo just one more button! All I could say to myself was *don't look, and don't let her catch you looking.* But it's like trying to tell a dog not to lick its balls I suppose! They can't help it, it's what they do!

She started off in a posh and authoritative manner,

'Good morning Chris, please call me J'

A man entered. He was about six foot, and I guessed around my age. He had jet black hair and boyish looks that made him look younger than he actually was.

'Chris, meet John Forester.'

He shook my hand with the usual greetings exchanged between us.

We were taken to an office that overlooked the old dry dock and a theme pub called the New Mount Stewart. It was an area that was buzzing years ago with ships being repaired so that they could travel the world. There were so many cargos: Tea from India and china, diamonds from South Africa, fruit, coal and wood from anywhere. Every journey was an expedition and an adventure. So much history had passed through those dock gates, now it was merely a few pleasure yachts where g and t soaked decks. What a waste! And such a shame! Is this progress?

He showed me to my desk and told me he had been with the company about a year. He stated that he was divorced with two boys. He only saw them at weekends as they lived in Bristol with their mother. We seemed to get on, and my impression of him was that he was a good guy.

Jayne (or J as she liked to be referred to) had lunch in the canteen downstairs with John and me. The company had their own gym, saunas and Jacuzzi on the ground floor; it was quite a place. After, we went back up to her office where she talked more deeply about the company,

'As you might know, my father, Sir Edward, set up the company quite a few years ago. He started off with a business called Heavy Haulage Overseas Ltd, which is now on the first floor of this building. Then he started a company called Rapid Cleaning Services Ltd, which is situated on the ground floor. He also established Edward Thompkinson Estimating and Engineering Ltd, or E.T.E.E. Ltd, which is the company that you now work for. Finally, the last company is E.T. Finance Ltd. That is situated on the top, or the third floor. My husband, Anthony, is in charge up there. So, as you can see, the whole organization is based in this building, hence the tight security. We have found that we require very few personnel to run this company. We like to keep it that way considering the nature of things that we deal with. As we explained in your interview, we are having to expand slightly due to demand. You already know we are a company that acts for insurers who want an independent estimation and an evaluation of damages. We ensure that our clients are not the victims of fraudulent claims. With your help gentleman, and your expertise regarding your engineering backgrounds, we shall keep growing.

Jayne sat behind the desk and looked up at John and me,

'I have been with the company for about twelve years, three of them as a director of E.T.E.E. I feel we have the start of a good team here and I am sure we will work well together.'

John smiled. I knew exactly what he was thinking.

'To start off, I would like you and John travel to Avonmouth docks tomorrow. You need to check out an insurance claim on a ship called the Eastern Diamond. The details are in this file.'

She handed me a red folder.

'I have to go to Swindon for a meeting with a Mr. Hutchinson. We are currently receiving about seventy five percent of our work from him, so I do like to keep him sweet, so to speak.'

John looked at me and raised his eyebrows. I choked back a laugh.

'You can pick up your car this afternoon. I will meet you the office at eleven thirty the following day for a report on what you have found. The ship's agent, Mr. Dennis Mackintosh, will meet you at the wharf tomorrow to show you around. The owners of the shipping line are not best pleased that we are involved with investigating them.'

With that we exchanged some pleasantries and she left. I picked up my Golf and asked John to take the company car home so he could pick me up in the morning. I walked into the flat and Sam was cooking one of her specialties, egg beans and chips. For a girl with an Asian background (and I really love Asian food) she is such a terrible cook! I washed it all down with a can of John Smith's to get rid of the taste. After, we settled down on the couch for the evening. We put on a DVD and cuddled. It was one of my old favorites: Blade. Who said that romance was dead!

Morning came too soon as usual. As I stood in the shower trying to wake myself up I heard the shower door move. Sam came in behind me, putting her arms under mine and across my chest. She pulled herself into me and kissed the back of my neck. We ended up on the bathroom floor in a very wet, slippery and tangled mess! I had to rush downstairs as a car horn was beeping outside. I was late.

'Sorry John, something big came up and it wouldn't go down!'

We both had a good laugh as if we had been mates for years. We chatted and chuckled about sex and women all the way to Avonmouth. We finally arrived at berth 5. In dock was a very grubby looking ship called the Eastern Diamond. The vessel was about a thirty thousand tonner, dirty white at the superstructure level and what I can only describe as a shitty brown color down to the draught mark. The deck was covered with forty foot steel containers. The cargo had been picked up in Gibraltar. A very short fat bald man was waiting at the bottom of the gangway. We parked and walked up to him.

'Hello, you must be J's boys. My name's Dennis Mackintosh.'

John stepped forward,

'Hello, we've come to inspect the damage.'

'Please come this way gentleman. As the ships agent, I have to be present when you inspect, for insurance reasons and countries legal jurisdictions. Just formalities you understand.'

He took us up the gangway to the forward hold where a twenty foot steel container had come loose in bad weather. It had smashed against the hatch causing quite a bit of damage. I walked up towards the container. Across the side was written Heavy Haulage Overseas Ltd.

'That's one of our company's containers isn't it John?'

'Yes Chris, we apparently use this shipping line quite a lot, our overseas department has a regular contract with them all over the world.'

I looked at the container and found that the shell of it had been smashed quite badly.

'Could I check for any damage inside Mr. Mackintosh?'

'I am very sorry but customs have told us not to break the seal on the door yet. This one is to be taken to the Bonded Store until they can look at it. I took a few measurements of the damage done to the hatch doors, bulwark and container. I also have some photographs.

'What is that smell?' I asked Derek.

'It's the cargo inside the hold, the hold is full of grain, and with the seawater going in it has rotted.'

The Captain came up to us and told us that they had to hold it down with chain blocks and Tirfors while in the middle of a storm. I finished writing in my note pad and we went back to the car.

'Do you fancy a nice heart attack breakfast from the Dockers canteen Chris?'

'O yes, greasy black pudding, eggs, beans, sausages and bacon, all washed down with a cup of tea, in a dirty chipped mug of course!'

We came out of the canteen full to the brim.

When we got back into the car I realized that I had left my measuring tape on the ship. We drove back to get it. I walked on board. Nobody was around so I went and got it. On my way back I passed an open man hatch. It was labeled No 2 Hold. Curiosity got the better of me and I looked down it. The smell that came from there was the same as number one hold. I climbed down the ladder and picked up some of the grain. I put it into my coat pocket. I looked up and noticed that John was at the top of the hatch. He asked what I was doing. I climbed back up to the deck and explained what I had found. We both checked number three hold.

It was exactly the same. I took another sample. As we walked back towards the gangway Mr. Mackintosh and the captain came out of one of the doorways leading into the ship's accommodation.

'What are you doing on my ship!' the captain shouted,

'You shouldn't be here, why are you sneaking around, what do you want?'

I told him that I had left my tape on board and I only returned to get it. On the way back to Cardiff we worked out our report. I typed it out on my computer at home. All I had to do in the morning was to get two ship repairing companies there to submit quotes for the job, do an estimation myself, and phone the Met office to check on storms at sea over the last week.

I went home and put my report on a disc, ready to take to work in the morning. I also put the evidence in separate plastic bags and labeled them for each hold. Sam came in acting like her usual bubbly self. We had an evening down at the local pub (we go there with her university mates). I got in much later than I should have!

Chapter 5

That noisy fucking alarm went off again! I had a little grump to myself before getting dressed and heading off to work. As I stepped out of the lift, J was waiting for me,

'I would like to see you in my office right away!'

I followed her into the room. She sat down, then went off on one,

'I was in a meeting yesterday with the Director of a shipping line insurance company. Funny enough the same people that insure the Diamond line of ships. They look after the Blue Diamond, the Yellow Diamond, The White Diamond, The Northern, Southern, Western and the fucking Eastern Diamond! Well anyway, a phone call was received from the Captain saying that you and John were on his ship without his authority. You had no right to return to the ship without his permission! It's registered in Panama and is not in British jurisdiction. He gave Derek such a bollocking over the phone and told me he would take this matter further.'

I looked at the floor.

'What were you thinking of? The instructions were to stay with Mr. Mackintosh at all times. You and John could have just cost us a major contract! I have worked so fucking hard to get this and you have fucked it up in one day! Get out of my sight while I decide what to do about this problem. Just go!'

Her attitude got my back up a bit, especially as I had a major hangover and I felt like shit. I placed my report on her desk and dropped the bags on top of it.

'Read this thoroughly, look at the samples then tell your Mr. Mackintosh what has been going on. The ship must have bought a load of duff cargo. They tried to avoid making a big loss, claiming for storm damage by using a container to smash the biggest hold on the ship. Oh, and by the way, go to the job centre and get another fucking idiot to work for you!'

I left the office and passed John. I told him that I would give him a call. I took a walk around the local park to cool down for a few hours then I went home. Later on, I picked Andrew up from school and took him to the local McDonald's for a treat. It was great fun being with him. We were laughing hysterically at a Simpson's DVD when Sam came in. I didn't want to trouble her with my problems. She had enough to worry about with her dissertation and exams. I took Andrew back home and parked the car outside the house in such a way that Jayne could see Sam in the car looking as stunning as ever. I know it's pathetic but it just made me feel good at the time! I dropped Sam off at her friend's to study for the evening and then parked the car up. As I walked up to my front door J came out of her car. She had been waiting for me.

'Hello Chris. Can I talk to you for a minute please? Can we go inside?' 'Five minutes' I said bluntly.

She took her coat off, threw it over the chair, sat down and began.

'Chris I owe you an apology. Look, I am so sorry. I know that I was in the wrong. I should have listened to you before I blew up. It was not something that I would normally do. I know this is not a very good excuse but I have a big problem. You see my Dad is not well. He has been diagnosed with cancer. They are treating him but things don't look to good at the moment, that's why I have been on edge. I am so afraid that I'm going to lose him.'

She placed her hands on her head and started crying.

'He's dying. Look Chris, I have promised Dad that I will keep the company going. Anthony is sorting upstairs out. I know that I am a good judge of character, and I am so sorry about yesterday. Even Mr. Hutchinson was impressed by your initiative and he wants to meet you. I need you back, but I need you to help me run the place. Chris, I will be straight with you. I had you checked out before you joined us. I knew you were straight. Dave would not have recommended you otherwise. Please help me. Obviously, I will up your salary and benefits. Please, just come back! With you and John running things I know that it will be in good hands. That way I can spend more time with dad. What do you think? Would you like some time to think about it?

'Can I just say something?'

She looked up at me; she had tears on her cheek. I handed her a tissue.

'Ok, I will come back and help, but if you get your arse in your hand again like yesterday you can forget it. Is that a deal?'

She agreed,

'I know it was a bit out of order but I told Mr. Hutchinson we would have lunch with him tomorrow. I hope you don't mind.'

I returned her smile.

'Come on, you look like you could do with a drink. Come down my local and have a quickie. You look like you could do with one!'

We went to the pub; she had a white wine and soda and I had my usual pint of beer, Brains S.A. (or skull attack as it's more commonly known!) We talked for hours about various things. She told me about the job, about how her mother had died when she was little and about her previous marriage that only lasted a year. I seemed to know everything about her after our conversation and I felt more comfortable with her. She told me that she always threw herself into work and didn't have much time for anything else. We got on all right, and by eleven-o clock we both had enough.

I put her in a taxi and arranged to pick her up in the morning. She left her black Merc sports car parked outside my place and gave me the keys.

CHAPTER 6

The meeting with Mr. Hutchinson went well and for the next month everything was great. I got involved more with running the floor and I enjoyed it. However, J's father was getting worse and he wanted to meet me (I suppose out of curiosity more than anything.), so one afternoon we left the office early and she took me there.

We joined the M4 heading towards the Severn Bridge and turned off on to the A40. After a few miles we traveled up a lane and arrived at a huge pair of metal gates. The pillars had huge lions on them. I could see a security camera either side of the gate and a security cabin hidden just inside amongst some trees and bushes. J waved to the guards inside as she drove past. We crawled up the driveway; it was lined with oak trees and must have been a kilometer long. It ended with an opening. The first thing I saw was a fountain in the middle of a courtyard which formed a roundabout. Ever since an early age all fountains ever did for me was to make me feel like I wanted to pee! It must be something in my subconscious.

The front of the house had Georgian style pillars, welcoming you to the two big hardwood doors about three meters high. I was amazed when I walked in. I think that I could have fitted my flat in the hallway!

'Dad has turned the library into a bedroom as he finds it hard to climb the stairs now. It's always been his favorite room. Don't be too shocked when you see him, he is very frail but sharp as a razor.'

A nurse came out of the room, said hello to J, and then quickly disappeared through another door. On entering the library I was astounded at the sheer size of it. It was wall to wall with books, from ceiling to floor. It also had one of those library ladders that move up and down the room to reach the shelves. At the end of the room was a big window that looked over an enormous garden and then down into a green valley with bluebells everywhere. Against the window was a bed with a drip bottle by its side hanging on a frame. On the bed was a very grey looking old man. We walked up to the bed.

'Hi Dad, I have brought Chris to see you.'

The old man smiled.

'So this is the chap that has been helping my little girl then.' He talked with an upper-class accent but his voice was strained. He raised his thin, weak hand and I shook it. He had a frail and cold handshake.

'Make us both a nice cup of tea please my love.'

As she walked out he began,

'It's nice to meet you at last. Please call me Edward. I don't think we need formalities! Firstly, I would like to thank you for your help, and from what J says I think you have a good future with us. Before she comes back I must ask you to please keep an eye on her for me. Help her through this, you see I haven't got long to go as you can probably guess, however I do have a lot of friends who care which helps. Anthony, her husband, dotes on her. He is such a good man.'

'You really don't have to worry about her. She is a very strong character! But I will help where I can.'

I replied,

'My old friend Dave was right about you. You see, he's been my guardian angel too on occasions. I know all about you and he has assured me I can trust you unquestionably. I am going to ask Anthony to introduce you to some of the other side of the business. He will show you how we are helping queen and country.'

Just then J came into the room carrying a tray. We had tea and biscuits and talked about future work. The door opened and a man walked in with a briefcase in his hand, he had light Grey hair which made him look very distinguished.

'Come in Anthony, come and meet Chris' said Sir Edward.

He entered, walked up to J and gave her a big hug and a kiss on the cheek. We shook hands and Anthony introduced himself to me. Sir Edward carried on,

'I have asked Chris to come along today. You haven't met before. There was no real need until now. There are a few things I have to put in place before I go'.

He looked at J and Anthony,

'Two of the most important people in my life are here and I need to know that this company will not take over your life as it has to mine. It has given me a good, profitable and eventful life but I need to know that you will spend more time enjoying life together and not spend your spare time at work. Everything will go to J and Anthony when I am gone. J, you will stay in charge. I am going to ask Chris if he would help out by running the company with you. I will hand all the top floor business over to my old MI6 friend David Denton to run. He will sort everything out for you. With the top floor handling some delicate matters we are obviously unable to sell the business. I would like Chris to work between the two companies as Anthony used to when I was there. You can load some of the responsibilities onto him, John also.'

Anthony pulled some papers out of his case and handed them to me. 'Chris, I would like you sign these, as from now on you will be dealing with confidential government contracts. You will have to sign this official secrets act. Tomorrow, I will show you around floor three'.

I signed the relevant forms and J took me back.

I got home around six thirty. Sam was relaxing in the bath with a book on the logistics of company law and its affects with something or other.

'That looks really entertaining Sam, get a life!' I said, as I exaggerated a very large yawn.

'Bollocks', came the reply with a smile. I took my clothes off and got in the bath with her. We had a laugh trying to make love to the rhythm of the moving water! When we got out the floor was soaking and had to be mopped up. Later, we opened a bottle of wine and settled down for the night with a takeaway.

CHAPTER 7

The next morning Anthony was at the office to greet me. We got out of the lift and he gave me a swipe card.

'This is the only way to get access to the top floor. Once you reach the top swipe it at the entrance. A guard is watching the lifts, walkways and corridors constantly. Security must be tight here, and if the card is lost, report it immediately. Fancy a cigarette?'

He handed out a packet of cigarettes, opened a door leading to the roof and lit one up. He put it between the little finger and ring finger of his left hand. He gave me a guided tour of the floor and stated that all the government contracts are handled up there.

'Come through here Chris, this is what we call the brain. It's our computer room'

I walked in and noticed that there must have been ten computers lined up.

'We have these linked to sites all over the world. We link up through the net. It's quite safe as we code all our signals in and out. Plus we have an amazing fire wall system. We look after problems that the government cannot be involved in. Some of these problems are very sensitive and cannot be brought out into the public domain. We also deal with countries that our government cannot be associated with. We send shipments all over the world. We have transported money, arms, food, explosives even a few people to different countries that were causing some major political problems. The damaged container that you were looking in on the Eastern Diamond was full of anti-tank missiles. The Captain didn't have a clue what he was carrying. He picked up the containers from Gibraltar on his way from somewhere in the med. You were right. Some idiot didn't shut the hold doors properly and seawater contaminated all his cargo, he didn't know about the other stuff. The best way for his company to get some type of compensation was to pick on the biggest hold and to damage it. He didn't know that he could have blown his ship and crew to bits.'

After our chat I was left with a lot to think about, and over the next few weeks I found it exciting getting involved with that side of the business. On the surface it all appeared to be above board but money in its millions was exchanged like confetti through internet bank transfers. We transported a shipment of currency to one country hidden in fifty-gallon drums marked up as vegetable oil. The money was printed in the U.K. then distributed to supply food and equipment directly to people living under a corrupt regime.

All of the operations on this side of the business had to be sanctioned and subsidized by a department of MI6. Information and finances were passed by a secure computer link to hundreds of bank accounts in different countries throughout the world. Sometimes money would change currencies by transferring through four different countries. Only Anthony and Nicky knew the codes, and whenever they carried out a transaction they would be sealed alone in a secure room. We laundered money that was collected from drug raids and deals and used it on the people it was taken from. It felt a bit like I was avenging Jimmy and Heike's death by getting at the bad guys. Anthony was a man who wasn't full of conversation but he did talk about him and J. John was a great help and much better company but as J's dad was getting worse she spent less and less time at the office.

The funeral for Sir Edward was a very solemn occasion. The people at the church included some very important government bods (some of which I recognized from the media). J and Anthony seemed to have a small family and only a few close friends. Sam came with me and J asked us both to go back to the house after the service. Sam was well impressed with it. We were introduced to her family and friends. Sam looked around the grand interior and asked J,

'What are you going to do with this place now, are you going to stay here on your own?'

J replied 'I have got so many good memories of this place. I don't think that I could even consider selling it, not at the moment anyway.'

I talked to Anthony for a while. I could see that he was watching over J, they seemed to be very close. As some of the guests were leaving I spotted a man chatting to J. I recognized him immediately; it was Dave! My guardian angel! I walked over and heard him chatting,

'Hello J, I am very sorry to hear about your father. I had the deepest regard and respect for him. He was a great man'

J affectionately squeezed his arm,

'Thank you Dave. Dad also held you in high esteem, especially after your time together in army intelligence.'

After the funeral, J had a few days off before returning to work. When she returned the country was on high alert. There were reports of a terrorism threat throughout to most of the western world. These people where using any means that they could to disrupt normality. We tightened our security even further. Everything was running smoothly until one of our consignments of arms went missing. We had originally "acquired" them from a raid on a Taliban stronghold. There were Kalashnikov rifles, mines, anti tank missiles and all sorts of ammunition to go with it. The official report said they where all destroyed but in fact were due to be sent to help rebels in a military coup somewhere in Africa. It went missing before it arrived at port.

The arms were in three blue steel containers and put aboard a ship which broke down near Morocco. All the cargo was supposed to be transported by three different ships in the diamond line to Gibraltar but the containers could not be traced. The whole situation was confusing, they could have been sat rusting at some dock in Timbuktu for all we knew. Two weeks passed and they still hadn't been found.

Anthony called a meeting with John, Jane and I. He wasn't in a good mood,

'All those guns and arms, how could they just disappear?' Until we find out what happened we cannot afford to send anything else. We have been told that an enquiry is to be carried out by MI6. Somebody could have intercepted our information, although that's highly unlikely. What's odd is that we fixed an EPIRB or beacon to all three containers and they have not been detected as yet. If there is a leek somewhere it is virtually impossible to be from here. We send information sparsely, and it is supplied on a strict *need to know* basis. I cannot believe that the leek has come from our side. It must have come from higher up. I am asking everybody to be patient until I know more. Please report to work as usual tomorrow but all ongoing assignments on the top floor are cancelled as of this moment.'

He left as quickly as he came in.

I went back to my office sat down, running things through my head. The door knocked quietly and Dave walked in. He put his finger to his mouth, beckoning me not to speak. He pulled a hand held device from his pocket and swept the room with it.

'Good this room is clean.'

He told me he knew that the three containers were going to be stolen. The Cheltenham spy centre intercepted a telephone conversation that had a key word which triggered an automatic trace on the number. The number came from the Hilton hotel, London. It was connected to someone on a pay as you go mobile phone (paid for by cash and no trace available). From the grid reference it was traced to this building. John came in to the room and closed the door behind him. Dave carried on,

'John was placed here to keep an eye on things but when you ran into bad luck Sir Edward helped me out. I didn't expect it all to go tits up but I can't afford to risk anything or anyone. This company has been infiltrated. I had the containers fitted with my own beacons before they left port. We had a tip off they would be lifted. Nobody will find them as they have been fitted within the shell and work on six hundred megahertz frequency that pulses once every hour on the hour for a one hundredth of a second so we can easily trace them. We will meet here again tomorrow at eight thirty. The top floor company is to be disbanded, but for the rest of the organization it will be business as usual'

CHAPTER 8

I must have got home around six. Sam was sat working on my computer. I put my arms around her and kissed her cheek. I suggested that she slip into something sexy as we would be going out. We went to an Indian restaurant on Witchurch road. We had a lovely evening. I had a chicken tikka buna and Sam had a prawn curry. We walked back to the car. We had a kiss and a cwtch under the warm glow of a streetlight then climbed into in the car. I turned the key in the ignition but it wouldn't start. I lifted up the bonnet, and with the light from the streetlamp glowing into the engine bay I could see a package wrapped in plastic with a couple of wires coming from it. One was wired to the earth connection on the battery and the other connected to an ignition feed wire. The twisted open wire looked like it had come apart, and the exposed bare wires had not joined properly, thank God!

I pulled the wires away from each other so that they wouldn't touch and pulled out the package. I looked inside and saw a detonator; there was plastic explosive inside. It was probably enough to blow up half the street. I stood there for a moment in disbelief, Sam broke my stare,

'What's wrong?'

'Nothing, I think it's a loose wire or something, I will be there now.'

I put the bomb under my jacket and put the wire back where it should be. I didn't want to go back to the flat that night, so I told her I was treating her to a night at the Marriott. As I got back in the car a set of headlights burst to life further up the road. A car's wheel-spun away in the opposite direction.

I couldn't believe it. I felt furious, but what could I do? My thoughts went back to Heike and Jimmy. We booked into the Marriot. I called J and John to tell them to tell them what had happened. I told Sam that I would be working away for a while, that's why I was treating her.

The following morning I went to J's house. I passed Anthony coming out of the driveway. He stopped and told me that Dave would be taking over the business, (apparently, it had been sanctioned in part of J's fathers will, should anything go wrong). Anthony was not happy. J was still in the doorway as I pulled up.

'My God Chris! What's going on?'

I pulled the explosive out of my pocket and explained again what happened.

'I'm going to the office. Look J, if somebody tried to blow me up last night? Be careful. Why don't you get away for a while? Book yourself into a hotel, stay low and I will call you later. Pack some stuff and get out of here for a while.'

I drove back to work where I found Dave sitting behind J's desk. I walked towards him in confusion,

'What's going on mate?'

As I got closer I noticed that he had a blank expression on his face; his eyes were open and he was staring into thin air. There was a line of fresh blood trickling down the side of his face. Looking closer I could see a small hole in the side of his head. He's been shot. My first thought was that the killer may still be here. I looked around and saw two small holes in the window. I ducked down low, turned toward the door and ran to my office. I thought that it would be safe as the window faces a different direction. From there I could call security then get the hell out of there quickly.

As I ran into my office there was an explosion. And that's where my story began, with me lying on my office floor and an armed guard standing over me.

I remember being taken to the hospital and feeling like death, wondering what would happen next. John was there to meet me. They put me in a private room with a guard outside the door. I hurt like hell and my ears where ringing like an old fire engine was in them. Luckily I had suffered pretty minor injuries considering that I was blown across the room: there was a nasty gash on the side of my head and some shrapnel had stuck in my stomach and ribs. John told me that he was keeping a close eye on Sam, Jayne and my son Andrew. He also said that the people who had shot Dave were also involved in events in Germany a few years ago. I was told to send a statement to the media, claiming that a gas leak caused the explosion.

We had a positive ID on three men caught on security cameras. One was the sniper, while the other two gained access to the building posing as repairmen and planted the bomb. They were both found later in a hotel room with their throats cut. The gunman was spotted on a street camera; it was Yip. I froze for a moment to catch my breath,

'How . . . ? He's supposed to be locked up!'

John told me that after the trial, Yip had been given to the Americans. He was due to be incarcerated in a high security prison called Pelican Bay in Del Norte County, California. However, the Americans thought that it would be more beneficial to do a deal with him, but he went missing from protective custody. Yip was working with someone that had info on our set up and we needed to know who.

The worst news was yet to come. Not only was Dave (the only man that had helped me over the last few years) dead, but Anthony had also been killed by the explosion. His body was blown to bits. He could only be recognized by dental records and his wedding ring. John told me that one million pounds had been paid into a credit Suisse bank in St Hellier-Jersey in Nicky's name. It was then transferred to a Swiss bank .com account. The account Number and passwords were found on her PC at home but she had disappeared, and so had five hundred thousand pounds in cash from that account.

CHAPTER 9

The next two weeks were spent recovering at a safe house in Bristol, working out our next move. J held a very private funeral for Anthony. I couldn't help thinking that there was not much of him left to bury. The poor bastard must have caught the full impact of the explosion. I was missing Sam. I wanted to see her and assure her that I would be back once all this mess was sorted out. John had arranged to have her picked up at the University and taken to a safe house in St Mellon's, near Cardiff.

I left Bristol with a couple of plain clothed security guys. We took the long route to get there, making sure that we were not being followed. We pulled down some narrow lanes that led to a farm house. It was set back from the road and sat on the cusp of a thick forest. They checked the house over before we entered. Blue Ford Mondeo pulled up the driveway; I could see Sam and John through the bay window of the house. They got out of the car and walked towards the door with John leading the way. It was so good to see her! I felt like she was bringing some sanity for me in this crazy situation. As one of the guards opened the door, then my feelings turned from joy to complete horror.

The guard behind him pulled out a gun and pumped two bullets into the back of his neck at point blank range. He fell outside the door. The gunman stepped over his corpse. I could see that John was trying to pull a pistol from his pocket but was shot twice and fell backwards over the car bonnet. Sam was in shock and looked straight in the eyes of the killer. I shouted as I ran from the window towards the gunman. I saw a flash and a split second later a loud bang came from his Browning. Her whole body flew backwards towards the car with horrific force. He turned toward me. I stopped about ten feet from him and froze. He grinned,

'Yip sends his regards! Any final messages for him?'

I could not make a sound, I just froze with fear. He raised his gun and I heard a shot. He fell to the floor. John appeared holding his side; one bullet had missed him and the other bounced of a rib. I ran outside to find Sam covered in blood. Her body twitched as she drew short, gasping breaths. Her big almond shaped eyes stared up at the sky into nothing. I took my shirt off to try and stop the blood from pumping out of her chest but it was futile. I kept screaming out,

'Talk to me Sam! Talk to me! Sam, come on! Sam don't leave me! What have you bastards done to her!'

I tried my best to save her. By the time that the Ambulance had arrived she had lost so much blood. They put a drip straight into her and didn't waste time getting her in the vehicle. The driver took off with a wheel spin, with me and the two paramedics working ferociously, trying to help her.

She died in the Ambulance. I could do nothing to help. I lay in bed in another safe house for a few days. I was numb, wishing that I had died with her at least I wouldn't be in pain that way. Half of me wanted revenge, the other just wanted release. I didn't feel strong enough to carry on. I was devastated.

John and J came into the room. I didn't want to see anyone. They didn't say a word for about five minutes then John sighed loudly,

'I am so sorry Chris'

'I want that bastard John! I want him dead! He's got too much blood on his hands. Will you help me?'

'First, I need to tell you something.'

J held my hand and looked back towards John as he leant on the windowsill at a funny angle. I could tell that his ribs were sore.

'I have asked J to be here because the three of us have the same common denominator; Mr. Yip. You see, we found out that J's father did not die from cancer, he was slowly poisoned. The outcome of the pathologist report showed it was a Ricin-based poison. It was administered slowly over a long period of time. The nurse who was looking after him has disappeared. We suspect that she was the culprit. We also found out that Heavy Haulage Overseas Ltd. was transporting drugs back into the U.K. We think that somebody in the company was using the system for their own personal gains. With Nicky and Anthony being the only people who had access to the codes it must have been Nicky all along. I want that man as much as you two. David Denton was not only my boss, but a good friend. There are only a few people in my department here that I feel I can trust. I don't know who has been corrupted. I have a proposition to make to you. I still have my contacts in the firm but they are based outside the U.K. David and I dealt with them in Asia. It's about time that I called in a few favours. I have had this idea passed upstairs to a high level. They are concerned that the recent events have tarnished their reputation. H.Q. wants this sorted out discreetly, for obvious reasons. I would like the three of us to work together to finish Yip off for good. There is an old saying that I think it's quite appropriate, "Don't get angry get even!" The team in Asia is working undercover and they have had no contact with head office. They only liaise with me and David. Most of the operation is already in place. You see, Mr. Yip has a history over there also. He is part of a group that is made up of triad gangs from different parts of Asia. They are trying to spread their wings and deal all over the world. I know that you had experience of Yip when you where in Germany. Now he has been given another area. It seems that he came back here to settle a few scores. The gang use the name "ren", this means knife in Chinese. The members can be spotted by a symbol that is tattooed to their ankles; (刃). The higher ranking members have gold rings with this emblem on. It will take a bit of time to set up. Think it over for a day or so but I promise you, we will get him!'

I gave John a steely look,

'I just want him dead'

John, J and I went to Nicky's house. We broke in to see if we could find anything. It was a small cottage in a little village near Cowbridge; quiet and tucked away between trees with a big garden full of all sorts of flowers in full bloom. We found nothing except an empty fridge and cupboards. All the furniture had blankets over the top of them. John and J pulled of the blankets and rummaged through the furniture. J and John found a Nokia phone down the side of the settee. The battery was dead on the phone so I put the Orange "pay as you go" sim card into my phone; it only had Anthony's number on it. He had sent text messages over a six month period telling Nicky of his undying love for her. Some clothes of his were in her wardrobe and there was a loose photograph of him in a pile of papers on the sideboard. This upset J. She turned away to conceal that her eyes had filled up.

'I just don't believe it. How could they! There is one thing that I want you to promise me Chris, when we catch up with her, she's mine!'

CHAPTER 10

Our first move was to disappear and make sure that everyone thought we were dead. This would stop any of our family being threatened; it would also give us some breathing space. However, it also meant that I could not have any contact with Andrew my son until things were over.

John's boss at H.Q. helped us to set this up as they wanted to get a result as much as we did. No one here knew anything of what we were doing. We took my V.W. Golf to a multi-story car park in Cardiff. I parked it on the roof level where it would be out of camera range and away from other cars. John followed behind in a plain white van. We planted three dead bodies in my Golf (they where freshly supplied from a motorway pile up on the M4). They had been taken from a crematorium and swapped with sheep carcasses to make the weight up. Our dental records had been changed also to verify it was us there. Due to nerves (and to try and bring a bit of humor to the situation) I told J her dental records had been swapped with the sheep and that we had to call her Baaaarbera from now on! She didn't even react. She didn't like any of this.

We struggled to put the bodies into the car, making sure that we left our credit cards and wallets with them. It was probably the worst thing that I have done in my life. I was sure the corpses were starting to get warm and gave off an unpleasant smell. It was an awful experience. J was sick over the back seat. The bodies had been dressed and the faces had tissue paper bags over them. I think if I had seen a face and thought of them as a person I could not have gone through with it. We placed balloons filled with propane in the car then disguised ourselves with hats and glasses so as not to be recognized should any camera happen to pick us up.

J and I walked down to the next level and out of the car park separately. John drove the van out after parking up for an hour in case anyone should check the cameras and times of vehicles coming and going. The car with the bodies in exploded into a fireball (after John checked no one was near) courtesy of the bomb left for me and Sam by Yip. John took the van back to the hire company and then we took trains at one hour intervals to Bristol Temple Meads. We booked into the Mecure Holland house hotel to clean ourselves up. None of us said much that evening. I think we were all in shock after what we had done.

The story was on BBC west evening news. That's when it hit home; Andrew and Jane would be informed about my death. The thought of them being safe was more important at that moment. The next day we took a train to St David's, Exeter. John took a taxi to a car hire company and picked one up using a false I.D. He collected us at the station and we drove down to a picturesque Cornish-fishing village called Mevagissey.

We booked into the Wheelhouse guest house on the front. John thought it would be better if J and I booked in as man and wife. John became J's brother. On the way down we went to Asda in St. Austell where we bought some clothes with cash.

While having a meal at the Ship and Anchor we discussed future events. 'Firstly we have to get new identities' said John as he was chewing on a piece of raw Sirloin dripping with blood. Nothing seemed to bother him.

'I have to visit a friend of my boss. He will get us I.D. It will be processed in the system to give us new N.I. numbers, Bank accounts and make us legit, at least in this country, should anybody decide to check. I'm also going to transfer money from Nicky's Swiss account to one we can access. A few hundred grand should fund us nicely. I will disappear for a few days and sort this out. I think that you will be alright; this is as safe a place as any. While I'm away just take it easy and relax as best as you can, from then on it will be down to business.'

John left, leaving us a pay-as-you-go mobile phone and a few hundred pounds in cash, reminding us not to phone anybody except him. We dropped him off at St Austell railway station and went back to the hotel for the night. The following day we drove to the Tourist information depot then headed for a little bay called Hemmick. It was a nice place to relax and just as beautiful as the brochure claimed. We sat and talked on the beach for hours. She talked about how much she missed Anthony and her dad and I went on about Sam and my son Andrew, wondering how and when I was going to see him again. Not being able to tell him that I'm alive was so frustrating and hurt so much.

The next few days went by very slowly. We drove around the coast and found some beautiful scenery. We walked to Dodman Point and back (which I think was good therapy for both of us). Each night we seemed to end up in the Ship and Anchor then crawl back to our room very drunk! I think we both needed it. By the fourth day I was feeling quite close to J and very relaxed in her company, it was more like a sister-brother thing though. I was feeling a little better in myself and my appetite was starting to come back.

John phoned to tell us that he had sorted things out and the next stage was about to start. I felt sorry that these last few days were going to end.

Cornwall is such a beautiful part of our country and reminds me so much of family holidays in West Wales as a child. I felt safe here and it was as if I was in a different world, escaping for a short while from the reality of what had happened. Strong feelings soon came back and I felt a lot of hate. The need for revenge merged with a feeling of uselessness at not being in control. I didn't like leaving everything up to John to sort out but I had faith in him, and (if he was anything like Dave) I was sure that he would be well on top of the situation.

J and I had a one last drink before stop tap then took a stroll along the breakwater, arm in arm. It was a clear night and the stars twinkled brightly above. We both felt safe. I think John knew what he was doing by leaving us there together, it was definitely good therapy for us after what we had been through.

John came back the next morning and we booked out of the Hotel. We drove to Manchester. To avoid being spotted together, J and I booked into the Cresta Court Hotel and John stayed somewhere on the outskirts. John had brought a case back with him; he opened it in our room. In it was a laptop computer with internet access and all sorts of paperwork. He gave J one pack and me another, explaining our new identities as he did so,

'You are a married couple called Jayne and Christopher Davies. Here's your marriage, birth certificates, passports, driving licenses plus bank account details and credit cards with pin numbers. There also a portfolio of your past lives. Fake of course, but learn it and then delete it from the computer as you cannot afford to slip up. If you make anybody suspicious it could blow the whole thing. My Name is John Davies. I am Chris's brother. I have come with you on holiday after leaving the navy. It's all in there so please study it and remember it.'

He passed the stuff to me. I found out that we had two hundred thousand pounds in a Jersey Account with debit cards to go with it.

'I have found out from a source that Yip has been sighted in Hong Kong. He was due to visit Singapore on business. He was caught on a security camera in a shopping centre. Our boys over there followed him to a café and had a long range microphone pointed at him. They overheard his conversation on the phone but they lost him in the crowd later. We know that he has family there and we have people keeping an eye on them just in case he contacts them again. I think the best thing that we can do for the moment is for you two to get out there and find a base in somewhere like Malaysia. Meanwhile, I will go to Hong Kong and see if I can find out anything else with our contact there. I will e-mail you and let you know the details. Oh and by the way the containers have been traced and it looks like they are on they're way to Asia'

We caught the early K.L.M. flight from Manchester to Amsterdam. About an hour later we boarded the flight to Kuala Lumpur. The thought of travelling on a 747 Jumbo in first-class for twelve hours was quite pleasant, not like the little Fokker that we had arrived from Manchester in! The journey seemed to last forever, but finally we arrived at Kuala Lumpar International airport. We were given immigration forms to fill in. We both ticked the tourist box and wrote down the name of the Concorde hotel where we would be staying. We then filled in the declaration of how much cash we were bringing in. We both had about two thousand Ringgits on us (with one pound being worth about six thingits as we called them!)

We took a shuttle from the satellite building to the main area. We walked up to the customs officer, who was sat behind a desk with a hijab scarf around her head. She looked at our passports,

'How long do you plan to stay in the country Mr. and Mrs. Davies?'

'We were hoping to stay in K.L. for a while and use it as a base to tour Asia.' J responded.

The customs officer interrupted,

'Have a good stay!'

I noticed that she stamped our passports for two months. We walked into the main foyer and up to the Concorde Hotel Kiosk. They took us in a big white Proton limo to the hotel. Outside was it was unbearably hot and sticky. We drove into the city. It took an hour to reach the Hotel (which is in the golden triangle area of the city, where three main roads make a boarder of shops and hotels.)

An Indian concierge came out to greet us. John was going to contact us the following day so we decided to look around the place and act like tourists. Just outside the hotel and around the corner was the K.L. tower. We went up it and found an incredible view of the City; the stainless steel of the Twin Towers shimmered brightly in the midday sun. To pass some time we also went to a Hindi Temple called Batu Caves (which was a hell of a walk up the 272 steps in the heat of the day!) There must have been about three hundred Monkeys running around and annoying the tourists but the temple was worth the climb.

We spent our first evening at a place called Bansar (an area of K.L. that seemed more like a U.K. town.) You could even get Caffreys on draught, but at a price of about Five pounds a pint (or about Thirty Thingits I think!)

That night we slept like babies and the following morning went down for breakfast. As it is a Muslim country they only served Beef bacon; it looked and tasted disgusting. Also, the milk seemed to have a funny after-taste. Luckily, there was a Hard Rock Café next to the Hotel which we frequented every evening. The food was superb, however, instead of the usual Hard Rock Pork Sandwich it was a Lamb one. The Malaysian and Chinese food was also superb and we were recommended visit the Old Stadium; the upstairs was an open restaurant. It looked like a naffi kitchen with huge cauldrons of boiling curries. It was the first curry house that I have been to which didn't serve Lager!

John called us in the evening. He said that he had been informed that Yip would be in Thailand within a few days. He was to swap stolen arms for drugs in a deal worth millions. The arms and explosives were due to be shipped to Pakistan, with the final destination being the Taliban in Afghanistan (Where they originally came from). Yip had the containers and was about to double cross the ren gang and swop them for drugs through a contact in Thailand. One of our sleepers found out about the deal and informed my boss.

He said that this type of thing had been going on for years. They are swapping drugs for guns and the drugs are somehow smuggled from Thailand down to Singapore. The Thai, Malay and Indonesian governments have a few officials who are involved and on the take. They fill a few palms with silver and turn a blind eye. There is an inbred corruption there, that's why we tend to work alone.

He stated that we must travel to the East Coast (to a place called Kijal) and book into a hotel called the Awana Kijal. It's about a forty-five minute taxi journey from Kuantan airport. We were to meet two contacts there that had worked with John and Dave in the past. His final comment was to avoid getting caught as we would be fucked.

CHAPTER 11

We arrived at the hotel and were amazed at the elaborate fountain that greeted us in the atrium lounge; with statues of dolphins squirted water out of their mouths. We booked in and went up to the room. The view of the South China Sea was incredible. A line of trees shaded a footpath that ran adjacent to a bright yellow sandy beach that must have been at least three kilometers long. The hotel was in the centre of a golf course which ran parallel with the beach. The grounds were all perfectly cut and manicured and Jungle surrounded the perimeter. J and I stared out of the bedroom window and admired this wonderful paradise.

The next morning at breakfast I passed on the beef bacon; I had toast followed by Cornflakes. The morning sun rose as I ate, erupting like a fireball across the South China Sea. Reception phoned our room and said that a letter had been left there for us. The note informed us that we must hire a car at reception then drive to a place south of Kijal called Cheratin. It was a twenty minute drive. Once there we were to find a bar called Jo's Beach Bar. We were to arrive by seven in the evening for a meeting. We put on plenty of mosquito repellant; an essential regime for the evenings there in Malaysia.

It was easy to get a car and the hotel sorted one out straight away. It was a white Proton Wira with air con and a steering wheel on the right side, thank God! We decided (after looking at the map) that we would take a drive to Kuantan and see what was there.

We went to a shopping mall and drove straight in to the multi storey car park; it had everything in it that a person could need. I was relieved to discover that it was fully air-conditioned! We went to the Cinema to pass some time then had food after. We couldn't decide whether to have a Kentucky fried chicken, a McDonald's or a Kenny Rogers Chicken!

We ended up with a Kenny Rogers Chicken. We talked about home and I couldn't help thinking of Andrew: I wished that he was with me. We drove back towards Cheratin and away from civilization. We passed lots of kampong-style wooden houses, some of them just looked like sheds but others were amazing. As we arrived in Cheratin we noticed that there were more tourists than locals! It was a back-packers haven. Something else struck me; it was like going back in a time warp! There seemed to be a lot of seventies-type hippy-looking dropouts around the place! We went to Jo's Beach Bar, and as we were early we took a walk along the beach.

The bay was a horseshoe shape with trees following its contour. The local boys were playing volleyball and showing off in front of some European girls there on a backpacking holiday (trying to add another notch to their kampong bed posts no doubt!) Finally, we traveled back to the bar. I had a bottle of Tiger beer and J had a fresh Mango juice. We weren't there long when a strange looking man and women walked in. The man was of European appearance, easy six foot two, quite slim and had not shaved for weeks. He had a pair of old sandals on (Jesus creepers I call them!), a pair of cut down jeans that looked like they hadn't been washed in years and a vest covered in stains. I hoped that he didn't smell like he looked! His companion looked like the kind of girl that you wouldn't take home to meet Mama! She was Chinese, slim, about five foot six with scruffy dreadlocks. I thought that her face and tatty jeans could do with a good scrub. She had a small moon shaped scar by her right side temple. She took out what looked like a joint from a tobacco tin and lit it up.

A guy at the bar looked at her with distaste. She just turned to him and said (in a well-educated English accent),

'And what the fuck are you looking at?'

The man looked shocked at her outburst and was taken aback. He turned away, shaking his head in disgust. She looked at me and I smiled (I thought that it was highly amusing!) she grinned right back. J stared at me with a bemused look on her face,

'Who's your friend?'

I laughed, saying jokingly that I have that affect on women! We watched as the couple took their drinks from the bar and walked towards us.

'Oh shit Chris, they are coming over here.'

'Don't worry.' I said, 'At least we won't need any more mozzy repellant on us, they won't come within a mile of them!'

We were still laughing as they pulled up two stools and sat opposite us. It turned a few heads at the bar. The girl spoke first,

'Hello Chris and J, John sends his best.'

To my surprise it was our contacts. I went to shake her hand and she declined. She said we were being watched by two plain clothed policemen at the bar. The guy said you can tell them a mile off; only a Malaysian copper would drink fruit-juice at Cheratin! He told us that they had been in Thailand for a while and had made contacts there. The local police were watching them like a hawk. It didn't matter though, he had found out all that he needed to know.

He had found out (through his contact at the K.L. drug squad) that his pad here was to be raided tonight as he had smuggled some Thai-grass across the border in order to get some credibility. He said that he would see us at the Awana hotel. After our chat they got up and left, kicking the stools over which they had been sitting on. I picked them up and bought another round of drinks.

As I was at the bar the plain clothed policeman approached me,

'They get all sorts around here. What did *they* want?'

I just told him that they were after money so I told them to piss off. I think that he believed me.

The following morning at the beach bar a crowd of ex-pat wives were having their usual morning coffee and chat. They were probably rabbiting on about the same subject that they discussed every week. They had nothing else to do out here. They were chatting about a man in the company that their husbands worked for, apparently he had been seeing a local girl and got up to all sorts of things with her. Lucky bastard! It was the highlight of my morning, listening to these women slagging of the guy. He must have been the envy of every ex-pat hen-pecked husband out there!

J went in the pool for a dip and I was lying there in a daydream.

'Do you mind if I join you?'

I looked up and saw a pretty Chinese face with a familiar scar. She had no dreadlocks today, just short cropped hair. She wore shorts and a Minnie mouse T shirt. I couldn't believe the difference in the girl. She sat down on the sun-bed next to me. She told me that her name was Lee. Both she and Steve (her partner) had been working undercover for the last year on a smuggling operation in this part of Asia. Through a contact in Hong Kong they had set up a huge shipment of drugs from Thailand to Malaysia which was about to take place. The drugs were to be used as payment for arms and Yip was involved. She informed me that I was to take on the role of an arms dealer, and that the final transaction would be completed in Singapore. The plan was to entrap Yip and the drug dealer. J came back from her swim and we went through everything. During this Lee was to stay at the hotel for a few days to keep J Company.

We went to a restaurant on the main road outside the hotel. There, Lee told us that she was originally from Hong Kong but as a child she had moved to London where her father owned a chain of restaurants. However, she did not enjoy the family business, and after university she joined the Metropolitan Police. She was transferred to the drug squad as she could fluently speak three dialects of Chinese, Malay and Thai. It didn't please her father much but she had worked hard and wanted to finish this case off for good.

Steve was a bit of an oddball. He had worked for the MI6 drug squad in London. Apparently, his partner had his throat slit whilst working undercover with one of the

Ren gang members in Hong Kong. He was a loner and had a tendency to sort things on his own. I was told that Yip watched as they killed his partner. When Steve found out that he could set him up he jumped at the chance. Lee told us that she trusted and respected him, even though some of his ways were a bit strange! I was beginning to feel confident that we could bring Yip down. After an hour or so we wandered back to the hotel and to bed for the night.

The drive to the North East coast of Thailand (via route three) was quite interesting. Malaysia is such a beautiful country; jungle, nice beaches and lovely people. I drove past some islands to the right hand side of me across the bays and they looked like an advert for a bounty bar! I remembered that the first bounty advert was made in Barafundle Bay in West Wales! It made me think of home again and how much I was missing Sam and Andrew.

I kept on route three and drove towards Rantau Panjang and the border crossing to Sangai Golok in Thailand. After about three and a half hours of driving I parked the car in a long stay car park that was just a patch of waste ground. I met Steve at a small café with Nasi-Goreng written above the door as pre-arranged. I didn't recognize him as he stood up to greet me. He was clean shaven and wore a small back pack, a bright blue and yellow Hawaiian shirt, white shorts and trainers. He said it would be better for us to cross the border together. Our cover story was that we were ex-pats taking a break from work in the Petronas Paka Oil Refinery.

The other side of the Malay customs cubicle there was a bridge crossing a river. We had our passports stamped and walked across it to the Thai customs. All across the bridge young boys were running up to us with umbrellas to protect us from the heat of the sun. They wanted small change in return. Steve shouted 'Mai' to them in a stern voice and they backed off, but still waited to be summoned like an obedient dog. The Thai side had lots of people begging on the streets (something that I didn't see in Malaysia.)

We went to the immigration booth and had our passports stamped then jumped on one of the many small motorbikes parked at the end of the bridge. John told the driver to go to the Marina Hotel and we set off.

CHAPTER 12

We drove into the Narathiwat region of Thailand and into the centre of Sungai Golok (which had modern buildings and hotels but it had a very distinct smell of its own!) After staying in the quiet jungle area of Malaysia it was a bit of a culture shock to enter this type of town.

We arrived at the hotel and were shown to our adjoining rooms. Steve came into my room and opened his backpack, pulling out a mobile phone. He then proceeded to take it apart and put the bits on the bed. He briefed me on our meeting with one of the dealers that evening; he was going to plant a bug on him. He pulled what looked like a grain of wheat from the bits on the bed and turned his phone on,

'This little baby is good for conversations up to about ten kilometers, after that distance it can be used as a beacon for up to one hundred K.'

He showed me how it worked.

'Look Chris, we have bags of time to kill. Let's get out for a while.'

We went to the fifth floor which was the health suite. The place was abundant with girls in masseur uniforms wearing wrist bands with numbers on. Steve walked up to the reception,

'Number Seventeen please for me and number Twenty one for my friend. I am in room 317 and my friend is in 319.'

He turned to me,

'Just relax for an hour Chris, it's a nice way to de-stress after a hard day at work!'

Number Twenty one came to my room. She was a good choice and certainly knew exactly what she was doing, twisting and clicking me into different positions before massaging me in places that only my mother ever saw when I was a baby! I met Steve later in the bar and he had a big smile on his face. I grinned at him,

'Feel better now mate!'

'Fucking marvelous!' he replied, 'living the dream mate!'

We had another beer just outside the hotel next to a stall that actually sold live Cobras. It made shivers go right up my back when I looked at them in their glass tanks. We had something to eat and he briefed me about the meeting again. We got the hotel minibus to drop us off the other side of town to a club with different theme bars on three levels.

We sat at a table and ordered our drinks. In an instant, girls surrounded us (I think they were anyway! It's hard to tell out there!), but when we said that we were not interested they walked away in disgust. On the stage dancers dressed in basks, fishnet stockings and high heels were teasing the audience on the front two rows with a raunchy number.

Steve told me that Lim had been involved with a triad gang in Hong Kong and had got himself in hot water with them for doing underhanded deals with rival triad gangs. He had to leave quickly or face having concrete slippers attached. He had settled down here and had a lot of gang leaders and police on his side after buttering them up. We had only been there for about ten minutes when four menacing looking Chinese guys in grey suits walked in and had a good look around. Two of them walked back out, the other two stayed and stared for a few seconds then sat down opposite us. One was fat and sat at the back and one was a younger, sleek looking guy. He stared at Steve,

'Nee hao ma Mr. Steven.'

'I'm fine Mr. Lim. I hope you are doing well.'

Lim just nodded. Steve carried on and introduced me to him. He shook my hand and passed a small bag of white powder,

'This is a sample of what you will be getting. Let's get down to it. You have something I want Mr. Chris. Please, I am a very busy man'

Steve handed Lim a list of arms and ammunition that had been stolen by Yip (as Dave predicted.) I told him in a stern voice,

'I am also a busy man Mr. Lim and I am sure we do not want to waste each other's time. I will make it quite simple. I have something you want and you have something I want. What we need to do is to get the quantities balanced so to speak. I have three containers with a mixture of Anti Aircraft hand held rockets, Kalashnikov rifles and enough ammo to start a world war. Look at the list'.

He looked for a while and responded,

'I will supply you in one delivery in Singapore, Top quality Heroin; 200kg. It would be worth about 15 million of your pounds with a finger value of 800 US Dollars. Diluted to finger value of 300 you will make a lot of money.

I realize that you have costs and I feel that I am being more than generous.'

After a while I sighed and shook my head,

'I am very sorry Mr. Lim. I want at least 350kg for what I have here.' 'Mr. Chris you insult me! My final offer is 200kg.'

I paused for a minute then looked straight at Lim,

'350kg Mr. Lim. I will be leaving in two days, please let me know your answer. And by the way, I know what you have been offered by Yip. Make your mind up and good evening.'

I walked out and went to the bar next door as we had pre-arranged. I sank a Tiger beer without even tasting it. I was still shaking with fear and hyped up with adrenaline when Steve came in a few minutes later.

'Nice one Chris! You deserve a fucking Oscar mate! He is totally pissed off! He told me that he wanted to slit your throat! He said that he would contact us tomorrow. I think we are pulling him in! Mind you, if he suspects us for one minute we will end up in a can of dog meat! What a way to make a living! We must keep on top of him and be careful. He wants a deal but he is a slimy bastard.'

One of the dancers walked past me, pinched my cheek and beckoned me to follow. Steve shook his head and laughed, rubbing a finger over his Addams apple. I got the message! We stayed at the bar and got quite legless after watching a talented local lady shooting a dart out of a piece of her anatomy that wasn't really designed for it! I shouted out,

'One hundred and eighty!'

We thought it was hilarious anyway! After, went back to our rooms and crashed for the night.

The next morning I was woken by Steve banging on my door,

'Chris, listen to this!' He played his mobile phone. He had planted the bug and had left it on record. The voice was in Chinese but he interpreted it. He said that Lim had the drugs hidden on a shipwreck called the Tasukete, just south of an island called Kapas back in Malaysia.

'We have to work fast. They are moving them in 2 weeks. We have to get back. I'll call Lee and J and have them meet us at the Marang jetty tomorrow. From there we can take a fast boat across to Kapas Island posing as tourists.

Lim caught up with us in the bar of the hotel that evening. He had his usual heavy mob entourage with him. We sat on a table out of the way, 'Mr. Chris, I will go with your deal, but first, are you sure that you can supply all of the goods on the list?'

'Mr. Lim, I am a man of my word. This amount of goods is not a problem. Please, if you think I am fucking with you I will leave now and no more said. If we meet in Singapore I'm sure you will be more than satisfied with what I show you, then we can finalize a deal there. Can we shake hands on this?'

He shook my hand and asked when he could take delivery. I told him that I could have it there in three weeks time. Lim then said,

'Mr. Steven has my number. I will see you in Singapore where we look forward to inspecting them. Goodbye Mr. Chris.'

He shook my hand and left. We went back to my room and listened in on the bug Steve had planted on him. He told his men that after the exchange we were going to be "dealt with" as he put it. We left Thailand that day (checking that we were not followed) and headed back into Malaysia.

CHAPTER 13

We met the girls at the Marang jetty which seemed about an hour and a half drive south from the Thai border. J gave me a hug. Lee went up to Steve and playfully hit him in the ribs, then walked straight past him and toward the boats. As she walked away I asked him what the score was between them. He told me that there was nothing in it but she was a great partner to work with. He also stated that I should not to challenge her to a drinking competition or a fight as I would lose hands down!

We booked a week on the island and appeared as two normal couples on holiday. The island Pulau Kapas inherited its name from the white beaches (it means cotton island in English.) The light sands on the beach were surrounded with palm trees. It was such a beautiful and remote place, I could almost imagine Robinson Crusoe being shipwrecked there. I had spotted the island on route to Thailand. It was definitely bounty bar advert scenery again but so unbearably hot. As the island had no electricity supply a generator would work from seven-o clock in the night until eight in the morning to keep the air-con working flat-out in our cozy wooden chalets. That evening we went to a restaurant owned by a very pleasant and helpful Malaysian guy called Rosman. We found out that his family had run the resort for ten years and that they also owned the Diving school. We talked to the girls about our Thailand experiences, (well, most of them anyway!) then we were all briefed on what was going to happen next.

We joined Rosman's Diving School and booked a course. Steve and I had dived before but as we didn't have legal passports, let alone certificates with us we had to do the whole thing as if we were novices. We went through the usual Valsalva movement to equalize the pressure of water on our eardrums. We went through buoyancy, sharing air underwater and mask clearing. It was a very thorough course (as they should be) and after our initial dives he had enough confidence in us to go a bit more into it. We dived in several locations around the island.

When we were back on land I saw a nautical map of the area on the dive shop wall. I noticed only one shipwreck on it. When I asked Rosman about it he told me that nobody was allowed there as it was an old World War Two wreck. It had been sunk five miles due north of the island by a British Submarine. As the vessel was covered in fishing nets it was not just dangerous; it was a designated war grave and apparently still had live shells on board. A few divers that had tried to steal relics from it had become fish food as they were blown to bits.

After a few days we were entrusted with our diving equipment and we took it back to the chalet so we could go for a shore dive in the morning. That's what we told him anyway. That night Steve had arranged for a boat to be waiting for us just out of site from the resort. We kitted up and left the cool chalet with the sound of the resort's generator humming away in the background. The pathways were lit up but we avoided them by walking around the perimeter of the camp and through the bushes, trying to be as quiet as possible. It was a hard task considering that we seemed to have a ton of diving gear on our backs. Small lizards scuttled in the bushes as we approached and luckily most of the noise we were making was drowned out by the generator and the hundreds of bats in the trees behind the camp.

The girls waited on the beach while we swam out. We kept to the left of the bay. By the time that we were around the headland it was pitch black which made it easy to see the lights on the fishing boat that Steve had there waiting for us. The lights from local squid fisherman's boats glinted in the distance. The three men on the boat greeted us and one of them was John. They had a small boat in tow with two people tied up in it. He told me that they were keeping an eye on the cargo and had been posing as squid fisherman. They would be kept out of the way for a few weeks.

Once we were in the boat he gave me a high five and a slap on the shoulder. It was good to see him and it brought back a confidence in me that had left with him. It took about thirty minutes to get out to the wreck. It had been buoyed and as it was such a calm night it was easy to find.

I checked my demand valve was working properly. Our air capacity showed that we had two hundred bar each in our twelve litre tanks with a depth of about twenty five meters, which gave me (with my breathing rate) about thirty minutes of bottom time. We dropped down to the wreck on a shot line John had positioned earlier. Steve and

I took the forward end of the ship and John and his buddy took the stern.

We dropped over the starboard side of the wreck to work our way from the sea bed up. A moray eel menacingly moved back and forth, looking at us through a hole in the netting hanging over the side of the ship. Luckily for us the netting had almost completely covered the bow area and it didn't take long to find a hole in it. I entered the hole, having a good look around with my torch for anything that looked nasty or that could bite me! I carefully went in through the hole. It was about a meter and a half diameter with very sharp edges. I could see right through into the chain locker.

It was very spooky inside the wreck, especially with a torch that only lit up where it was pointed. It didn't seem to throw out much ambient light in the surrounding area either. The water temperature was colder within the hull and it gave me a shiver through to my bones. I think it made things worse that I was on my own in there. My imagination was running riot with what I thought I could see in the shadows. Old chains where piled up on top of each other forming rusty pyramid shapes in a small chain locker area. No sign of anything nasty though, thank God! Fish were swimming around me and a quite large moray eel swam quickly past me, making my heart race with fear and my breathing somewhat faster than usual. John came in through the hole which made me feel better. All around the floor net bags lay there, weighed down with old chain links and lead weights. I shone the torch on my hand and gave an O.K. signal by bending my index finger to touch my thumb. I got out of the black-hole feeling very excited. It was like I had just found some long lost Inca treasure.

I inflated my delayed submerged marker buoy (DSMB) and sent it to the surface to signal we found something. I put some air in it. It started off slow and then sped up; it was like a rocket, shooting to the surface as the air expanded in the long thin cigar shape float. I was warned that these should be let off from a maximum of ten meters because whatever the reel is attached to sticks, (and you have hold of it) you could risk a bend by being pulled up too fast to the surface.

The boat dropped a mesh cage down beside the line and we started filling it up with the net bags, then we surfaced. It is a totally different world underwater, especially at night. All you can hear is the noise of the bubbles rising around the side of your head and boat propellers (miles away probably). You don't have a clue which direction these noises are coming from; it's a dark, alien environment. It made my senses heighten more than I could have ever imagined, it was so exhilarating! We got back on the boat and pulled up our bounty. We cut one of the nets open to reveal a sealed plastic bag which was what we had hoped to find. Everyone on deck was in high spirits.

Steve and I were taken back to the island, then John and his crew went back to get the rest of the bags. John told me later they had more than three hundred kilos of heroin from there. It must have taken them all night to get it out. When they had finished John planted some explosive and a detonator to go off in the bow of the ship the next day. This would hopefully put Lim off the trail of thinking that someone had stolen his stash.

We swam the last 100 meters back to shore and the girls were there waiting for us. We sat on the beach and sank two bottles of Tiger beer, then sneaked back to the chalet and had a few more drinks.

The next morning at the Diving school we swapped the empty cylinders quickly without anybody noticing. We did not have a dive that morning which left a space of twelve hours since our last dive. The gap made sure that the build-up of nitrogen in us was minimal, preventing us from getting the bends. At the end of that day we took the boat back to Marang and then headed south back to Kijal and the Awana hotel.

CHAPTER 14

'Well, we have started the ball rolling guys!' John said as he sipped on an ice cold fresh Mango juice. The five of us sat around a table at the poolside after a very relaxing breakfast watching the plain back (or pegu) sparrows fly around the open air restaurant, cheekily stealing any leftovers. John carried on,

'Mr. Lim won't be too happy about his stock! We have arranged a meeting with Yip in Singapore. That gives us enough time to relax for a few days and get ourselves together.

That evening we went north of our hotel in the car for about thirty minutes, straight through the jungle and Kampon areas towards a glow in the sky that turned out to be the Petronas oil refinery. All this hi-tech equipment on the edge of jungle, it seemed funny that bottled water was more expensive than petrol there! We stopped at a place called JR's where we had pizzas and Carlsberg lager on draught (that went down very well!)

It was a restaurant that had an American type bar through a doorway on the inside. The place was air-conditioned and had all sorts of flags and beer mats from all over the world on the back wall behind the bar. There was even a Brains beer mat and a Welsh flag there! It was probably a gift from one of the Welsh ex-pats.

While at the bar all sorts of people were coming and going; British, Australian, American and a few very loud Germans came in also. One of the Germans kept bumping into Lee (obviously drunk) and repeatedly asking her how much it would be for an all-nighter. She moved away from him but he blocked her way. He had obviously said something else to her. She grabbed hold of his nuts hard; his face was a picture of sheer pain and surprise. His mate came across and was about to push her off him when Steve (who was an arms-reach away) tripped him in such a way that he fell into his chest, then he applied a strangle hold as if it had been rehearsed a million times.

'Move and you're fucking dead!'

This guy was choking and Steve held him with just enough pressure to deter him. Meanwhile, Lee had let the guy go and shouted "Prick" at him. He raised his hand to her, which was probably the worst thing he could have done! Before he could do anything she had struck him in the throat, kicked his leg and thrown him to the floor. She triumphantly stood over the German guy, goading him to get up. Unfortunately he tried, and as he rose she threw a roundhouse kick at his face. It connected with a dull thud, knocking a few of his teeth out. He collapsed in a bloody mess on the floor.

We paid up and left just in case any police were around. When we got back to the hotel we had a drink in the bar. J was still a bit shaken from the incident but Lee and Steve didn't even mention it. I said to Lee,

'You're a bit handy, wouldn't want to mess with you!'

She grinned,

'They see a Chinese girl here in a bar with westerners and automatically think she's on the game, pricks!'

I was glad to have them on my side.

At the beach the next day J and John (who seemed to be getting on quite well) had gone for a walk on the beach. Steve was doing his Norman no-mates stroll up the beach and Lee was lying on the bed next to me. We had a good conversation about home and what we would do when we returned. I liked her and thought that she was totally out of place involved in this situation, probably as much as I was. We went for a walk and met J and John coming back. We both had a backward look as we passed each other and smiled. It was good to see that J seemed to be happier. I didn't think that she should be out here either but it was impossible for any of us to return home, not for a while anyway.

I took Lee to Cheratin for the evening. Steve was on another one of his wanders back in KL and J and John seemed to want some privacy together. We kept away from JO's bar and found one that had a live band playing Santana's music; it also had a good menu. We even got up to dance. Nobody would have recognised her. The scruffy girl that I bumped into not too long ago had transformed herself. She wore a tight fitting pair of jeans, a pair of light khaki colored canvas walking boots and a plain white blouse opened to the fourth button down. She looked gorgeous. We got back to the hotel at about twelve. I walked into the room and caught J and John together. I just coughed out 'o shit sorry' and closed the door. Lee said, 'You had better come and stay in my room tonight'

Being a bit drunk I gave in gracefully! She walked into her bedroom, took off all of her clothes and then run the shower. Halleluiah! She was up for it!

'Fancy a shower? It's been a long hot day!'

I couldn't believe my luck!

'You go first if you like' she said. I had my shower while she was watching CNN on the telly; more soldiers had been killed in Afghanistan fighting the Taliban. I can't help feeling for the families and loved ones who are left with an empty void that can never be filled. I take my hat off for these brave people fighting for a free world. What state would the world be in now if it was not for these heroes, past and present.

I jumped into bed and called to her,

'There is only one bed here so I hope you don't mind sharing'

After a few minutes she came out of the bathroom with only a towel around her and jumped in beside me.

'I don't know quite how to say this but, well . . . it's not that you are unattractive or anything but I . . . how do I put it . . . you're not my type. I prefer women to men'. I felt like I had been slapped in the face with a wet echo. She jumped into bed and turned the lights and the telly off.

'Only joking! That had you didn't it! You should have seen your face!' she started giggling like a school kid. I called her a bitch and laughed,

'How could you do that to a man!'

We had a giggle about it then things got a steamy!

The next morning at breakfast was strange. One of the maids saw John coming out of my supposed wife's room and me coming out of Lee's. We made a joke of it but it was a stupid thing to do. If curious eyes had noticed us it could have been dangerous. We agreed to be more discreet from now on. I told Lee about Sam and my life, she told me more of hers. I did feel as if I was betraying Sam's memory but I promised myself that I would get revenge for her Heike and Jimmy.

We had a meeting to start the next phase of the plan. We all sat in the foyer of the hotel out of ear shot of any passers-by. John sipped his coffee,

'Let's start from the beginning. We have got Lim's drugs but he doesn't know that. The containers with the guns and arms have been traced with the beacons Dave planted on them to a ship docked outside Singapore harbor waiting to be let in to port. Now we need to meet Yip and his Ren gang to set the next phase in motion. We have to move from here. It will probably better to move to K.L. for a couple of days. J and I will travel to Singapore to set things up. We will move Lim's drugs to a steel container and booby-trap it, just in case someone decides to take them. In fact, it will have detonators built in so if someone opens the door and doesn't tap the correct code within sixty seconds there will be nothing left but a crater peppered with flesh and metal.

He handed out mobile phones to everyone. They had all sorts of gadgets in them. We could talk to each other at the same time like on a conference call, and we could also trace each other with an in-built sat-nav system. Also, there was a camera and two bugs in each phone.

'Chris and Lee will be better off out of site for a while. They will book in the Legend Hotel in KL. We won't need you pair until the final op. Steve is going to sort back up. He will meet us in Singapore, but J and I will go on ahead first to set things up.'

CHAPTER 15

We drove from Kijal and the lovely Awana hotel to Kuala Lumpar where we booked into the Legend Hotel. The road to KL from the Genting Highlands was very twisty and a civil Engineers nightmare but an amazing sight. It was a road that I imagined you would see Jeremy Clarkson from Top Gear powering down, screeching around the bends in a bright red Ferrari soft-top. As we drove down it the twin towers came into sight, it was well worth the drive.

We had to take a lift up to the hotel; it was on top of a big shopping complex. As we walked into the main door somebody was playing a grand piano in the foyer. Our room overlooked the city with the Twin towers stainless steel shell dazzling the city in the midday sun.

That night we went to the Monkey Bar upstairs. It felt like we were on holiday together and I thoroughly enjoyed it. We went to the Bansar area for a meal and afterwards more sex until we fell asleep.

The next morning I wondered what the hell we would do in KL to pass the time. We had a great time. She was a bit of a gym freak and really liked a good workout. She looked good working out too! She used the hotel gym and finished her training session with a swim and more sex. I don't know where she got the energy from! We had a phone call from John after three days. We were needed in Singapore. He had already booked the tickets and we arranged to meet him there.

The flight lasted barely an hour and on arriving we took a taxi straight to the Concorde hotel, not far from the famous Orchard road. It was so different to the Concorde hotel in KL. This one had glass lifts inside the building that went up all the way to the roof. The building was round in shape and the rooms formed a circle around the perimeter, with a big empty void all the way up the centre to the roof.

We arrived early in the afternoon and decided to have a drink downstairs in the bar; a Philippine band played to a very small audience. My mobile rang, it was John. He told me that the plan had changed a bit. Yip wasn't coming himself but someone would be taking his place. The meeting had been brought forward to tomorrow at noon, and as Yip was not there to recognize me, so I could be used as back up.

We all met that morning to discuss a plan. Steve arrived at the Raffle's restaurant fifteen minutes before the meeting was due. The place was a history lesson in its own right! The entrance to the hotel had an Indian concierge dressed in an all-white uniform and turban. He greeted everybody on arrival as they got out of their taxis. It was a fantastic periodical white building and well deserved of the old phrase of the time: posh (I read somewhere that it derived from: Port out Starboard Home which applied to the rich, first-class passengers travelling on ships in those days before air con, not having the sun beaming into the cabins.)

Black wrought-iron greeted you as you entered the main foyer area. The reception area was carved from hardwood. It was a real colonial example of architecture. It was quite different to its surroundings. In the hotel arcade was a stream of designer shops and a restaurant which was to be our meeting point.

To disguise myself a bit I had grown some stubble. I also wore a baseball cap and dark glasses. Lee and I sat at a corner table in the Tiffin room and ordered a famous Tiffin afternoon curry with a couple of drinks. There were only a few people in there and they all seemed to be dressed like tourists. I thought that we blended into the background well.

We waited for about ten minutes before a lone man wearing a light cream suit walked in and sat next to Steve with his back to us. I didn't get a good look at him as his panama hat was tilted slightly and dark glasses covered his face. He had a European look about him. He took off his hat and glasses and turned to address the waitress.

He talked to Steve for a while and drank a glass of juice in between conversations. Steve was bull shiting him, saying that he would buy at a better rate than Lim. They batted figures around and he seemed interested. Steve handed him a wrapped box of chocolates with a sample in. He picked up the box and left. Outside, he lit up a cigarette. He put it in between the little finger and wedding ring finger of his left hand. It seemed familiar. Then to my horror I recognized him, it was Anthony, J's "dead" husband! I have never seen a ghost look so well! I gave Lee a shocked glance and she got the message, she already knew who he was. She whispered to me that we would talk back at the hotel.

The trek the hotel along Orchard road was murder in the sticky heat. When we entered the air conditioned room it was such a relief. Lee sat down on the bed and told me that they had only known for a short while that Anthony was alive. Steve had told Anthony or Ying Guo (English) as he was known here, that the goods were already in Singapore. He went for it hook, line and sinker. I was suspicious. How could J not know that Anthony was alive? Was she in on it? She seemed to be genuine, especially seeing how she grieved for Anthony. I thought that it would be a good idea to keep a close eye on her anyway, just in case.

Steve and I arrived at the Hard Rock café after another hot and sticky walk down Orchard road. Lee followed behind checking if we were being stalked by anyone. We walked up the steps to the entrance and were greeted by a waiter with a menu in his hand,

'Have you booked sir?'

I told him no, and asked if we could have a relatively private table as we were expecting guests. Almost as soon as we sat down Lim walked in with one of his stocky Chinese gorillas. He sat down,

'Nee Hao ma Mr. Chris. I am here as you requested. When and where do we exchange?'

'There is a problem. We have been offered a better deal. We met some people you may have heard of called Yip and Ying Guo, and they have assured us . . . '

Before I could finish my sentence he flared up, ranting in Chinese that I didn't understand, except for hoon dan I think it was.

'You bastard we already make a deal! I hope you not go back on your word!

He thumped the table with both hands aggressively. As he did I threw a clear plastic packet full of his heroin on the table. It was double the size of the sample he had given me in Thailand. I looked at him, acting as if I was really pissed off at him and growled at him in a low but aggressive way. 'This sample was from Yip. I have had it checked and amazingly its quality and make up are identical to your sample. What is going on Mr Lim? He is ready to exchange. What is going on?'

He answered quickly, too quickly,

'I sold him a load last month'

Steve got up and told him that he was obviously lying and the deal is off. I got up and Lim shouted,

'Qing Zuo Xia! Sit down please and I will explain! I have had a consignment stolen, I know it is him but I have a lot more stock. He is obviously trying to fuck with both of us! I will deal with him!'

'This is purely business to me Mr. Lim, I do not want complications. I can hand him to you as a goodwill gesture. The deal is that I get my stuff and you get your arms. I do not intend to get involved in your private war. You can do what the hell you like with him, I really don't care. What confuses me is that I thought he was an arms dealer, not a drug runner, but I will make a deal with you. If I lead you to Yip, and what he stole off you, I want an extra thirty thousand in American dollars, as a goodwill gesture.'

'I will be more than happy to help!' He said, shaking my hand and looking deeply into my eyes as if he was looking for a sign of me lying. I tried to remain as cool as possible,

'I will call you soon Mr. Lim, Good evening.'

CHAPTER 16

In a quiet corner of a jetty in the East Lagoon Tanjong Pagar Container Terminal, by the three giant cranes, the three blue steel containers that held the guns and ammo that Yip had stolen where on board a ship that had just docked. The containers traced by the beacons planted were unloaded and the Singapore police had arrived to take them back.

The police had paid off two of Yip's guards; they reported in every four hours by radio. They were promised immunity in exchange for providing evidence of Yip's illegal operation. Their other option was to receive a mandatory death sentence for trafficking.

The green container full of drugs that we had stolen from Lim had been placed alongside the containers of arms to make it easier to keep an eye on them all. All of them were wired with explosive and would explode if opened without the correct pin number being tapped in to the control box (which was screwed to the inside of the door as an extra security measure.) Steve, John and I arrived at the main security gate of the docks. We showed our (fake) passes to get us onto the site. We walked into the office near the containers and pointed a gun at the two guards. We knew that they were also working for Yip after some mobile phone tapping by the police. We gagged them and tied their hands together.

Steve had already contacted his boss to get some help from the Singapore Police; they took them away. The Commissioner had sent the Singapore S.T.A.R. team (or Special Tactical and Rescue Team.) They dressed all in black and were armed with black HK-MP5 sub-machine guns and Israeli 9mm Jericho pistols. They were very organized. Steve had talked to their commander, and as a result eight of them had been positioned around the site as back up for us. They had also previously searched the area for any gang members and had hidden two snipers atop the cranes, just in case it all went tits up.

Steve called Lim and gave him directions to us. Lim arrived with five of his men in an articulated lorry that had a steel container on a trailer with more of his heroin in. It shocked me that he could get his hands on so much stuff in a short space of time. Steve and I walked up to Lim. We shook hands and Steve was handed a backpack with a pile of US dollars in it. I opened it, counted it and nodded at Steve who walked up to one of the containers full of arms; he opened it. Lim nodded his head at his men and they pulled out guns, clicked of the safety catches and pointed them at us. Steve shouted at Lim,

'If I don't put the correct code into this keypad in sixty seconds we will all be blown to pieces!'

Lim laughed,

'Then we will all see heaven a little earlier than expected!'

The beep coming from the box was getting faster as the time for detonation was getting closer. Steve ignored Lim, walked up to the box and tapped in the code. The box stopped beeping immediately. Steve shouted at Lim and his men,

'Lower your weapons!'

Lim looked at both of us shaking his head and laughed. Steve pointed at one of his men and then touched his right arm. Out of thin air a bullet hit Lim's man in the arm. It ripped through the top part of his right arm; flesh and bits of T shirt exploded from the exit wound. As the bullet left his body it ricocheted off the tarmac, hitting the container door away from us. He contorted from the force of the impact and dropped to the floor screaming in pain. Lim's men raised their guns and frantically scanned the area.

Steve then pointed at Lim,

'You want some of that!'

Lim glared at Steve and told his men to lower their weapons. The Star team came out of hiding with their weapons aimed. They shouted for them to drop their weapons in both Chinese and English. Four of the Star team kept their HK-MP5's pointed directly toward their prisoners as three of them put cable tie hand cuffs on them. The captives were then pushed to the floor, face down. The wounded guy lay there holding his arm while one of the Star team kicked his pistol away from him. Another Star officer picked it up. They had no option but to surrender. The first stage of our plan had worked! Lim and his men were taken away in custody by the Star team.

Steve called Yip and said they would meet at the Keppel terminal later. J turned up with Lee in a taxi and we all waited in one of the container offices, out of site. Steve went to pick up Yip and Anthony and bring them back. He had activated his phone while driving them back and we heard Anthony and Steve talking. I couldn't hear Yip's voice. I looked at J to see if she recognized Anthony but the line was not that clear. I wanted to warn her before they arrived but it I also wanted to see her reaction. The car pulled into the yard and drove toward the containers. Anthony and Steve got out of the car. Yip wasn't there.

Steve had told us to come out of the cabin as soon as he arrived. As we walked towards Anthony, (who had his back to us) J looked confused. She walked right up to him and stared into his face. She slapped him hard and just stared for a while,

'What the fuck is going on Anthony!' she screamed at him while her eyes filled with tears. She seemed to get over her initial shock and attacked him, shouting, kicking and screaming. She was either a good actor or genuinely shocked from the way she had reacted.

Anthony pulled out a gun when he realised that he was caught. Steve raised his hands and four armed men came into view. He told Anthony not to be stupid and beckoned him into the security office. I was closest to Anthony and he handed me his gun. We all went into the cool air-conned cabin.

J started shouting,

'Why Anthony! Were things really that bad? You murdered my Father you bastard! You poisoned him! Why? And as for Nicky, where is she? I want to know where she is!'

He sighed heavily,

'Do you know how hard I worked for your father? I was never good enough for his little girl, I wanted more out of life than working twenty four seven for that prick! To make things worse, Dave simply walked in and took over! That job should have been mine! Look, I can give you a lot of information but you have to give me something back. What if I give you all the Ren members? There are many diplomats working for Ren members all over the world. You set me up with money and a new ID and I will give you all you need.'

John replied,

'We did not have a clue that you were alive for definite until you showed up at Raffles. How much did you get away with, two maybe three million? But that's not what we want. You will be working for us over the next few months. When you're finished, and if you're lucky, then we might send you away somewhere nice. If you don't we will let you go and inform Yip that you are working for us and always have been. All we want in return is for you to give us Yip'

He contacted Yip on Steve's request and arranged for the two of them to meet at the dock. They were to depart tonight (along with the containers) on one of vessels that Yip had on his pay roll and travel to Hong Kong.

One of the Star team injected a bug device into Anthony's arse cheek. Apparently, it would be good for at least three months and could be traced over a hundred kilometers. The green container of drugs was loaded onto a ship called the Hao Yun. The arms containers where to be sent to a high security holding yard and placed aboard a U.K. navy supply vessel, destined for rebels fighting Gadaffi's regime in Libya.

After he had issued the instructions, Steve took Anthony back into the town and dropped him off. By the time that we got back to the Concorde J was in a mess. I tried to comfort her but she was inconsolable.

Anthony confessed that Nicky had been killed, and that he had buried her near to her cottage. He planted evidence to throw everyone of the trail (and did a good job of it.)

Anthony had even sourced a stand-in body for himself; he and Yip had planted it before the explosion. That's why Yip was spotted in the building.

Lee finally brought J around by explaining that nobody had a clue about Anthony until Singapore. None of us wanted J left in the U.K. on her own; she was very vulnerable and would not be safe there. I was annoyed that Yip had once again escaped our grasp. I hated him, and each day I wanted him brought to justice more than ever.

CHAPTER 17

Steve had been told to take everyone to the Pan Pacific Hotel. We went to the loft suite were Steve introduced Michael; his boss at MI6. He was well groomed and in his late forties. Judging by his stature he was physically fit and obviously ex forces. He talked very abruptly and carefully chose his words. He thanked everyone for the work carried out. He said that some Hong Kong government officials were Ren members. Their aim was to take control of the underworld from the triad gangs, which themselves had grown in number since Hong Kong was handed back from the British.

The British government had felt partly responsible for handing it over with major triads like the Wo Shing Wo and Sun Yee On gangs still very active. With our cargo being sent there, the drugs would be used as a "sprat to catch a mackerel" as he put it.

I could not take any more of this crap. I stood up,

'What do you mean? Yip goes free? It's not good enough. We have all put ourselves on the line for you! We have lost too much to just sit back and watch him literally sailing away into the fucking sunset! He murdered friends of mine and you think I am just going to let him just go!'

I threw my glass of water at the wall in temper. Steve's boss butted in, 'You should be aware that this operation is much bigger than you! We had knowledge of someone in the company giving out information and we did not know who. We got things wrong and thought that Nicky was the key. Anthony did a good job setting her up. We need the big fish, and this deal has pulled them all in. We now know the identities of most of the Ren members here and in Europe. Thanks to all of your efforts we nearly have them, but we have to lure the Hong Kong members. By sending this ship to Hong Kong will pull them out of the woodwork'

I got up and looked at Michael. I shook my head in disgust and left the room. John, J and Steve followed five minutes later. J was spitting feathers about it all and said that she had enough. She was going to the airport to fly back to the U.K. I offered to take her there but she was adamant that she wanted to be on her own. I gave J a hug before she went and told her that I would call her when I got back. I wanted to stay and get Yip. I slipped a bug on her from my phone to make sure that she got to the airport safely. Lee insisted to take her to the Airport and finally J gave in. Everyone was pissed off with the situation.

Three hours had passed and I still had not heard from Lee, I was getting concerned. Michael called Steve to say that Anthony's bug has confirmed the Hao Yun had left port and he was on it with the containers. I turned my phone on and activated the bug that I had planted on J. As soon as I turned it on I heard Anthony's voice,

'Yip, fancy a drink my friend? It was a bonus Lee taking you to the airport! We can use her as a bargaining chip if we need to. The longer they take to find out Lee is missing, the better. I have missed you so much J' 'Me too! You wouldn't believe how hard it's been. I am not looking forward to spending days on this rusty old tub.'

Yip laughed,

'At least it's not for long. Why choose North Vietnam to sell all this shit Anthony?'

An American voice butted in,

'You know the good old U.S. of A has been helping to disrupt things there for awhile to some of our rebellious friends. We have been doing it for years.'

Anthony interrupted him,

'They have given us a good deal. Anyway, we leave port for North Korea tomorrow at nine a.m. I have locked Lee in the fore peak rope store. There will be a guard with her at all times. She won't get out of there. If she is not needed when we get to our destination we can throw her into the ocean. By the way, my arse is killing me! Was the guy who removed the tracking device from it a butcher?'

Yip carried on to say that the bug and the container were on the Hao Yun sailing for Hong Kong; it would "accidently" sink on route. The American guy butted in again,

'Yeah, sorted by Uncle Sam of course! Well, with a little help from MI6. They did just gave you away and expect us to just lock you up, lucky that they didn't know about our arrangement! I hope that you enjoy your retirement after this drop off Mr. Yip. It's been good doing business with you!'

We all looked at each other. The phone sat-nav system showed us that J was close to the Tanjong Pagar Container Terminal where we caught Anthony. We listened for a while and discovered that they had moved the cargo to a different container. They had loaded the container on the Hao Yun and loaded it into a different container and simply took it back off the ship. The container was then moved to the vessel that Yip, J, Anthony, the American and Lee were on. We had to move fast.

Steve was about to call his boss Michael, I stopped him and reminded him that they would just let Yip go again. We all got into this to get Yip, and we had an opportunity to end it for good.

CHAPTER 18

John called a friend in the Singapore drug squad and convinced him to pretend that he had received a tip-off from an anonymous caller. As we approached the ship I didn't even take note of the name. J's bug was coming through clearly and we found the vessel straight away. We had waited until it was dark and met the Singapore police at the harbor entrance; they had borrowed a local ship repairer's mini bus. We all got on board wearing boiler suits, hard hats and work boots. Three plainclothes police men walked up the gangway in front of us, cursing in Chinese that is was a bad time for the generator to break down.

As we came to the top of the gangway the police took care of two armed men. Two officers kept the guards at bay while one other policeman and John went to get Lee. More plain clothed police in a van pulled up and walked up the gangway. Steve and I walked into the main corridor through a watertight door. We were holding toolboxes and pretending to look for the engine room. We found the Captain's cabin easily and I knocked on the door. I tried the handle but it was locked; voices murmured inside. I knocked the door and mumbled some gibberish, making sure that I would be heard inside the room. Someone shouted in Chinese. As the door opened my silenced Walther P22 delivered two rounds directly into the forehead of Yip. As his twitching body fell back I pushed the door hard to get him out of the way of the door. Steve and I both ran into the room. The American went for a shoulder holster; Steve shot him in both arms, then in the head. J and Anthony looked pretty shocked. I told them to put their hands up. Outside it sounded like world war three was starting. Some guy burst in shouting and panicking; Steve shot him twice. Anthony rushed toward me. I managed to shoot him in the shoulder. He landed on the floor as I let two more shots off into his head.

'That's for Nicky you prick!'

I shot the Captain, picked up the American's gun and put my gun in his hand to make it look like he did it. All this time Steve kept his aim on J. We had to leave and quickly. Steve looked at J,

'Sorry, no witnesses'

He shot her twice in the head and put his gun in Anthony's hand. I picked up a notebook computer from the desk that had a dongle attached and put it in my pocket.

We walked back the way we came in. The gunfire had ceased but loud shouting in Chinese was coming from all over the ship. I walked out of the door onto the deck and was thrown straight to the floor,

'Don't shoot him! He's one of ours!'

One of the police officers helped me up. I could see Lee and John down on the dock side getting into a police car. John's police contact told me that they would destroy the drugs once the media had been informed of the haul and how good a job the Singapore police are doing. He told us to leave immediately and shook our hands, thanking us for our assistance.

Later that night we all went to the Crazy Elephant Bar at Clarke quay to de-brief. We sank a few bottles of Tiger beer. I was so glad that Yip was dead but it did not make me feel the way I thought it would. I had so much hate for him . . . so why didn't I feel some kind of elation? I consoled myself with the thought that he would never be able to hurt anyone else.

CHAPTER 19

The next morning I picked up the New Straight Times, the headline read: *Singapore Police Foil Major Drug Deal.* A sub-heading below stated that a container ship named Hao Yun had gone missing in the South China Sea. The story reported that it was carrying a cargo of unstable chemicals which exploded. No wreckage or survivors had been found but a search was being carried out. A British Cargo ship reported seeing a bright glow on the horizon. Apparently the American Navy had sent two ships that were in the area to help with the search.

The next day Steve's boss visited us while we were having lunch; he was furious. He had found out (via the Singapore police) about the switch and he knew that we had something to do with it. We all looked at each other blankly and acted dumb.

Since this whole nightmare was over, Lee and I decided to go back to the U.K. to see our families. She had not seen them in a while and I wanted to see Andrew. We landed at Heathrow and arranged to call each other that night with some pay-as-you-go phones that I bought. I hired a car and drove down the M4. It was so nice to drive over the Severn Bridge and see the *Welcome to Wales* sign.

I drove to Jayne's house and knocked on the door. It was Saturday lunch time and dickhead answered. Jayne came beside him; they were obviously very shocked to see me! She cried and gave me a hug. Andrew must have heard my voice and he ran into my arms. I held him so tight and I didn't want to let him go. I could see that Jayne was pregnant. I was pleased for them and I thought that it would be nice for Andrew to have a little sister or brother. We all went inside. I told them that I had been working abroad for the government and that I had been forbidden to contact anyone. Andrew and I spent the afternoon together. We went to the cinema at Nantgarw and after I treated him to bowling and a McDonald's. He was going on holiday for a fortnight with his mum the next day. They wanted to take a holiday before the baby arrived.

As I drove through Cardiff memories came flooding back; of Sam and what had happened to me. I did not want to stay here on my own without being able to see Andrew. I wasn't sure what to do next. Everything seemed to be an anti-climax and I felt so alone. Maybe I was just tired and burnt out? That seemed like a good analysis as I had lived on nerves and adrenalin recently.

John split the money that was left in the account which he set up when we started the operation. He said that the money was written off by Her Majesty's government as a thank you for services rendered. The money from Lim had been handed to the Singapore police. I still had the laptop and the dongle from the ship. I found out that it contained details of a Swiss bank account. I intended to look into it when the heat had died down!

I called Lee. She said that she was delighted to be home and intended to leave the drug squad. I arranged to drive up the next day to see her and spent the night in the Cardiff Hilton. I didn't sleep much, despite the amount of Brains S.A. that I sank at The Old Arcade watching The Cardiff Blues and the Ospreys battling it out on the field.

Lee and I booked a flight to Majorca for a few weeks relaxation. She told me that she was going to stay in the U.K. to help her father manage his restaurants. She even offered me a job washing up!

She told me that the Hao Yun (Yip's decoy container ship) was torpedoed by an American sub. It was sunk north-east of the Macclesfield bank in very deep water so that nobody would find it in a hurry. It was nice of them to do our dirty work for us!

Lee and I had a great holiday and decided to give a relationship a go. Her Dad wanted to expand his business and he offered to set Lee up. She had found an old pub that was shutting down near the centre of Cardiff and bought it to open as a restaurant which meant that I could be close to Andrew. John had gone to stay with his brothers in America for a while and Steve had gone on one of his walkabouts to Canada but kept in touch through his hotmail account.

Things were going well for us. Three weeks after we opened the restaurant John sent me an e-mail on a hotmail account we had made up and one I only accessed from a phone registered to a dummy address. There was an attachment to the email and he had written bellow. Do not open the attachment unless you do not here from me in one month and don't tell Lee unless a month had passed. The problem is that I'm an impatient nosey bastard!

. . . Why did I look?

Lightning Source UK Ltd.
Milton Keynes UK
UKOW04f0315280913

218111UK00001B/20/P